ALIEN DOMINATION

Long ago mankind realized their dream and reached out to exploit the stars. In the form of a race called the Delikon, the stars reached back in anger.

As earth ships had damaged strange worlds, so alien starships punished earth. It couldn't really be called a war; it had lasted less than a day. When it was over, earth's starfleet was destroyed. After chaos had reigned for a week, the new overlords landed.

With each new generation, humans were allowed to forget more, until there remained only myths of past terror and power, the temples and the Ruling House.

THE DELIKON

H. M. HOOVER

AVON
PUBLISHERS OF BARD, CAMELOT AND DISCUS BOOKS

Cover illustration by Sharron Vinston.

AVON BOOKS
A division of
The Hearst Corporation
959 Eighth Avenue
New York, New York 10019

Copyright © 1977 by H. M. Hoover
Published by arrangement with the Viking Press.
Library of Congress Catalog Card Number: 76-54271
ISBN: 0-380-40980-1

First Avon Printing, November, 1978

AVON TRADEMARK REG. U.S. PAT. OFF. AND IN
OTHER COUNTRIES, MARCA REGISTRADA, HECHO EN
U.S.A.

Printed in the U.S.A.

One

IN A NORTHERN LAND stood a palace encircled by the arms of a gentle river. To the east were temples; to the west, cypress-guarded tombs. A white road led to the river and crossed the high bridge.

In the palace gardens were reflecting pools and an enclosure for tigers. Three children played in the garden; Alta was ten, Jason was twelve, and Varina was three hundred and seven.

The tigers heard the approach before the children did. Behind their moat, on sun-warm rocks, the cats awoke to flick their tails in irritation. Their great eyes narrowed, and their ears went flat. From west to east, high above the mountains, a brilliant object streaked across the sky, slicing through cirrus clouds, trailing a wake of white vapor and silence.

"A meteor! A meteor!" chorused two of the children. But Varina said nothing. She watched the fireball until distance dwindled it to a bright speck lost in the clouds, and her face, which had glowed with the pleasure of the ball game a moment before, went still.

"What is it?" said Alta, seeing her friend's expression change. "Did it frighten you?"

"It's just a meteor," Jason said reassuringly. "Nothing scary."

"One of the gardeners says meteors are bad omens," said Alta. "He said something bad happens every time one comes. . . ."

"Excuse me." Varina thrust the red ball into Jason's hands. "I must go . . ." For a moment her strange cinnamon eyes scanned first Jason's face, then Alta's, as if she had never seen them before and might never see them again. Then she turned and ran down across the lawn and disappeared behind the hedge of the topiary garden.

"Are you coming back?"

She heard Jason call, but she couldn't answer because she did not know.

The gravel pathway scrunched beneath her boots. Her running stampeded the herd of tiny deer feeding along the river bank, and panicked peafowl from their dusting holes. The covered bridge boomed as she raced across it, passed the guardhouse without a word or glance at the sentry, and sped on up the slope toward the temples.

The sentry, made uneasy by her haste, looked after her and then walked halfway out on the bridge to make sure nothing was chasing the child.

Although she had run more than a mile by the time she reached the temple courtyard, Varina was not out of breath, but her face was flushed and her eyes were very bright.

"Sidra!" she called on entering the courtyard. "Sidra?" The goldfish in the fountain pool fled into the shade as her shadow passed over them. "Sidra?" There was no answer. The fountain gurgled; the flowers glowed; a wren sang a sweet brief song. She hurried along a path of flagstones embedded in moss to a door in the garden wall. "Sidra?"

A servant appeared with startling suddenness. "The t'kyna is in the temple," the servant said with a bow. "The t'kyna ordered us not to disturb . . ."

But Varina did not wait to hear the end of it. As she ran out of the courtyard gate, from somewhere within the great building she heard a bell tone sound and knew Sidra had been warned of her approach.

The woman met her on the steps to the great portico. She was dark and tall, with an aquiline grace that had in it something vaguely alien. When she raised her hand to order Varina's silence, sunlight flashed off the emeralds that adorned her long, tapered fingers and gleamed on the gold webbing of her belt as she turned and led the way to a secluded spot.

6

"Now, with what excitement do you disturb the servants? What is it that could not wait for twilight?" Her voice was low and clear, almost without feeling.

In spite of herself Varina felt a tiny stab of fear, and suddenly what she had run so far to say didn't seem that important.

"I— I saw them," she said rather lamely. "They are coming back."

"You saw them? Whom did you see?" It was apparent Sidra knew the answer, but she wanted it confirmed.

"I saw the starship."

Sidra absorbed this in silence, her gaze occupied by the distant view of snow-capped mountains.

"Does this mean it is ended?" Varina almost whispered the question. Sidra's glance met hers, held, and softened.

"I am sorry," she said. "I should have told you. They will be here tomorrow."

Two

LONG AGO mankind realized their dream and reached out to exploit the stars. In the form of a race called the Delikon, the stars reached back in anger.

As earth ships had damaged strange worlds, so alien starships punished earth. It couldn't really be called a war; it had lasted less than a day. When it was over, earth's starfleet was destroyed; random cities were made deep pits of fused glass, all orbiting and surface craft incinerated, all power sources shut off. After chaos had reigned for a week, the new overlords landed.

Throughout the world the alien conquerors dissolved all boundaries, all customs, all laws, and imposed their own. To restore and enforce order, the Delikon established unique military bases staffed by their creatures, whose appearance became the stuff of nightmares.

7

The universities were closed; technologies destroyed. Newspapers and video broadcasting of current events ended; too much awareness was disorienting to humans. New laws regulated dress, language, and behavior. A firm caste system was established, with clerical families, factory families, musician families, farming families, mining families, and so on, from which the individual could escape only by a series of tests. All belonged to the State. All was controlled by the State.

The Delikon were powerful enough to be benign where practical. Since the planet remained overcrowded, those who wished to emigrate were encouraged to do so. During the Era of Emigration, millions of potential colonists left earth for new worlds. Apparently they found what they sought. None ever returned. That they had gone was forgotten.

Those of the Delikon who remained to rule earth underwent the structural changes necessary for adaptation to this foreign world. But one adaptation they could not make, and, in time, their failure to do so made them suspect to some and venerable to others: No human ever lived long enough to see an alien die, or even age. Those few alien children who came to earth remained always children; those who appeared elderly lived on. Human life span was too brief to measure the age of the Delikon.

Because it appeared to comfort these creatures of earth, the Delikon allowed those who wished to worship supernatural beings to continue to do so. In time they even built them small and lovely temples as places of meditation. (The aliens were religious in a manner not understood by humans, alien perception having been expanded by the vastness of that small portion of the universe the Delikon had traveled.) As humans forgot and dissimulated their fears, they came to regard the aliens themselves as supernatural humans and erected temples to them.

Generations passed. The starships came with less frequency. All but a few of the alien military bases were closed. With human breeding strictly controlled, vast cities emptied and were razed. Part of the earth grew green again. Forests returned, but there were new deserts. Rains washed soil off entire mountain chains to reveal skeletal rock.

With each new generation, humans were allowed to forget more, until there remained only myths of past terror and power, the temples, and the Ruling House. At least once in each decade, the shuttle of a starship not of earth came and went from an isolated and highly guarded peninsula along the northern sea. No human ever saw its passengers or freight, and those who saw it entering or leaving the atmosphere failed to recognize it for what it was.

The Delikon conquerors had chosen to preserve several hundred square miles of the least ravished sector of the fragile planet. Around its mountain borders they built a secure boundary across which nothing passed without permission. In the northern uplands they built Kelador, the Ruling House. To Kelador they brought the best of what remained of the lifeforms of earth and the artifacts of man. They also brought human children to be trained as administrators of the world the Delikon had subdued.

Delikon children were never seen outside Kelador. They were brought to the conquered planet as teachers, for among their own kind only the minds of the young remained resilient enough to endure constant contact with the human mind.

The Delikon had quickly noted the illogical human desire to idealize those they found physically pleasing. Therefore, they took great care in choosing their future human administrators from all levels, but especially those who would one day serve as governors. Like Alta and Jason, all were dark haired and golden skinned, children in whom the genes of earth's divergent peoples had blended to a catholic beauty. All were intelligent, fine boned, and slender. By the time they left for the academy, there was about them an aura of innocence, general good health, and the gentleness born of self-assurance.

Yet, beside their teachers, they appeared merely handsome. The Delikon took special effort when they restructured their teachers. Varina was an ultimate tribute to their technical, biomedical, and mechanical skills. Her one imperfection, the large, oddly colored eyes that could not be altered, somehow made her more humanly appealing—that, and the fact that in her long exposure to the human children with whom she lived, she had perhaps absorbed more of the alien mentality than the Delikon technicians· had counted on.

Varina had come to Kelador before any living human could remember. It was she who first trained generations of administrators; she who taught the basic simplicity of cosmic order to the human children whose world was limited by the boundary of Kelador; she who made them love and trust their overlords and truly believe in their own eventual right to rule and enforce the edicts of the Ruling House.

Once the children left their young teachers to enter the academies, they were forbidden to return to Kelador until their lives had served a purpose. And if they longed for the ordered peace and beauty that was once theirs, then it was their duty to re-create such an atmosphere somewhere in the sector they were eventually to rule. Then, and only then, could they return.

It was Varina's duty to inspire this dream. Because she did it more successfully than anyone else, she had suffered for her competence by serving nine times the normal period of enlistment.

Three

"I AM AFRAID," said Varina.

What might have been either surprise or vexation briefly crossed the woman's face. "Of what?"

"I do not want to go back. . . ."

10

"Your devotion to your companions is well known, Varina"—Sidra sounded impatient—"your ability to identify, touching; but you confuse affection with duty. Admit your duty to this pair is ended. Next week they leave for the academy. If they ever return to Kelador in their adult form, they will be as foreign to you as your past students have been—and as pompous in what they imagine to be their success."

Varina looked at the ground and drew a circle with the toe of her boot.

"I meant that not as cruelty but as simple fact." Sidra spoke more gently, and, taking Varina's arm, said, "Come, we will walk in the gardens."

They went down the broad steps in silence, and, as they crossed the plaza, a servant hurried toward them from the courtyard. Across his arm he carried their capes to ward off the chill of approaching evening. Varina accepted hers with a smile of thanks. Without slowing her pace, Sidra lifted the garment from the extended arm and no more acknowledged the servant's presence than she would a piece of furniture. She flung the cape around her in a shining swirl of green. "We will take the lake path."

Varina had suspected they would. She knew Sidra's fascination with the tigers.

"Now. Why this fear? Is it the restructuring? There is no pain."

"No. Not that. I had forgotten about that." But thinking of it now added to her unease. She had taken this body for granted for so long a time. And there *was* pain—she remembered that and thought perhaps Sidra had forgotten. But pain was not what she feared.

"It . . . I have been here so long . . . if I return no one in my House will remember me. I do not remember them. Not really. In the time passed we have shared nothing. To them, I will be a stranger with five fingers. . . ."

"Admittedly there will be an awkward period of acclimation." Sidra's tone suggested she did not consider it a serious problem. Then, pointing to the lake's mirror surface, "Look at the evening star gleaming in the water—the graceful black curve of the rush above it."

Varina obediently glanced at the reflection, but her mind was distracted. Was Sidra listening to anything she said? They walked in silence for a time until they reached the stone wall surrounding the tigers' moat.

"You will readjust to your House."

"But *this* is my home. . . ."

Sidra ignored the interruption and went on. "Once you are gone from here your own intelligence will remind you of the obvious—that here you are truly an alien in an alien land; that these people are to you as their cats and dogs are to them—beloved pets to be cared for and trained. And as man lives many times the life span of his pets, so we live many times the life span of man."

"Alta and Jason are my friends, not pets. They are equal. . . ." From a nearby tree a peacock gave a mad, mocking scream, and she started involuntarily.

"Now—perhaps. As all the others once were. Remember?" said Sidra. She smiled appreciatively as one of the white tigers rose from its place on the rocks, stretched, yawned, and then sat to wash itself like a common house cat.

"Regard the tigers, how they ignore us. We saved them from extinction; we house, feed, and preserve them for generations. But they are above gratitude. They ignore us. If they could, they would kill us. They know there is no basis for friendship between us. We shall always be alien to one another. So it is with our species and man. But I much prefer tigers. Recognizing my prejudice makes me more tolerant of man than I otherwise might be."

As Sidra watched the tigers, so Varina watched her. "Have you never felt anything for any of the people here?" she asked hesitantly. Sidra was her guardian, but she was also t'kyna, and one did not ask one of her rank impertinent questions. But Sidra answered as to an equal.

12

"Yes. In the beginning. Even though I had been warned by my predecessor." She gave a very human shrug of apology. "They can be very charming. I know. Very endearing. Especially when you consider their vulnerability to us. . . ." For a moment she seemed lost in other times, old memories. "But then you learn they are charming with motive—usually to gain power through your weakness for them. They can be very skillful manipulators. But it was the few who never disappointed who caused the most pain. Because, you see, you miss them so when they die." Her eyes clouded for a moment, then refocused on Varina. "I no longer allow myself the luxury of being charmed by any other than our own kind. It is too enervating and serves no practical purpose. Nor will I allow it to happen to you again. I have long protested your remaining here, and I have finally won. You will return with the ambassadors, Varina. There will be an earthwide turn-over rotation of almost fifty. Your situation is not entirely unique. My chef is going home; she has been here since the beginning. And Malik has headed the treasury almost as long. I shall miss you all."

Four

AT DAWN, for the seventh time in that century, a long convoy of heavy vehicles snaked its way up through the mountains and approached the Great Gates of Kelador. Noiselessly, the gates swung open. The convoy rolled through, unchallenged by sentries, human or otherwise. The sun's first rays gleamed on the cars' domes. None could see what rode inside.

Like a train, or one creature, the vehicles moved perfectly spaced at a synchronized speed. Steep grades, switchbacks, hairpin curves, all were negotiated with no visible braking or gear changes. The sound of rolling wheels on pavement was constant and echoed through the mountains in a dull roar.

High on a rocky ledge, beneath a sheltering cliff, a solitary rider sat and watched the convoy pass as he shivered in the mountain cold. He was clad in common garb, his hair tousled and his face dirty. Yet for all this apparent poverty, he rode a fine horse and his boots were glove soft. The binoculars he used were monogrammed, and his hands, though grimy, had recently been manicured. Like a sentinel or spy, he watched the cars until they disappeared from sight in the pass that led to the foothills.

The cars sped on through the pass and down the forest road to the plains where the great herds grazed. By midmorning, they had reached the farm lands and villages that supported and were in turn supported by the Ruling House. The rooftops of the town of Vale came into view, and on the distant peaks the observatory and relay-station domes winked in the snow. They passed the military base with its blank façades. No traffic was encountered. All had been ordered off this road. The convoy slowed once; a woman and a little girl stood by the roadside. The child carried flowers. Both waved, and the woman held aloft an object of veneration. The convoy did not stop.

At the palace only a very select staff was on duty; all others had been given long-scheduled holidays and were absent from the palace grounds. All visits, official or otherwise had ended several days before. In the green room, Vashlin, chief administrator of the Ruling House, and Sidra, t'kyna, liaison to the High House of D'laak, patiently awaited their visitors' arrival.

In the clock tower, Varina, Alta, and Jason waited, Jason with a pair of high-powered binoculars trained on the distant highway. They had slipped out of their apartments in the palace and by back hallways and great stealth arrived here long before dawn. They still wore their capes as protection against the chill winds from the mountains. They shivered occasionally, as much from excitement as from cold.

14

With a whisk of wings folding, a gray pigeon landed on the north ledge behind them and was closely followed by a second. The pair of birds peered into the dusty dimness of the tower room and discussed in anxious coos the presence of visitors. Deciding the children were harmless, one bird became distracted by the sight of its own pink feet and stood lost in meditation of their wonder. The other, losing patience, flew up to an unkempt nest on a ledge beneath the roof and was greeted by the excited peeping of young.

"They're coming!" Jason announced. The whine of heavy motors became noticeable in the distance as the convoy drew near. One by one the domed cars appeared between the trees, turned right to cross the high bridge, and moved slowly up the curving driveway to the palace steps.

"I never saw cars like that!" whispered Jason and pointed. "Look what they've done to the drive!" The gravel had been crushed to sand by the weight of the cars.

"Keep away from the wall," whispered Varina nervously. "We might be seen."

There was the riffle of a small motor. A triangular shadow raced down the steps and over the lawns as a monitor craft flew overhead and circled wide above the river. A squadron of armed sentries in dress uniform issued from the palace and positioned themselves on the steps.

With a hiss, the lead car's double doors opened, and the opaque dome split to slide inside itself and reveal the shaded interior. There was a flash of brilliant green, and a form filled the opening and emerged onto the steps. As the ambassador stood erect, Varina felt a sense of shock. It had been so long since she had seen them in their natural state.

Even from this height it was apparent the Delikon was larger than any man, and its movements, though easy, suggested great weight. The head was encased and concealed by the bubblelike helmet that gleamed gold in the sunlight. Wind billowing the green cape

15

revealed a bare upper torso of burnt sienna flecked with iridescent gold. With one long arm, the Delikon reached to adjust an apparatus worn on its belt and then closed the beautiful cloak around itself more tightly, as if chilled.

Behind, a second Delikon emerged from the car and stood for a moment, getting its bearings. Its bubble helmet sparkled in the sun as it turned slowly this way and that. And Varina knew that under that bubble, great cinnamon eyes were unblinkingly registering even the most minute items within a mile range. She had forgotten they all had equal vision.

"Get back!" she whispered urgently as she pulled the children into the shadows with her. They were staring with open-mouthed wonder. She could not blame them. The Delikon looked alien even to her. She had not seen them since she was ten of their years—had been deliberately kept from seeing them all this time—until she had almost forgotten what she had been and knew only what she was now.

They would change all that, as most of the Delikon arriving now would be changed by week's end. They would look terrestrial and she would look . . . she held out her hands and stared at them wonderingly; they had served so efficiently. It seemed a shame to alter them.

"What are they?" Alta managed to ask. "They're not . . . people . . . are they?" Varina missed none of the fear lurking behind that careful pause.

For a moment cinnamon eyes met brown. They are *my* people, Varina thought, but she did not say so. And now, to save herself the pain of seeing her companions become frightened of her after ten years of trust, she avoided the truth.

"They are Delikon," she whispered. "They are . . . quite remarkable."

In the distance the tigers began a coughing roar. The alien scent had reached them on the wind. From below came a series of sounds, unrecognizable as words, but interesting.

"I want to see what's happening," Jason whispered urgently. "Let me go," and he tugged at her grip on his wrist.

"No. Stay back—it is unsafe. They have eyes like my . . . they will see you."

There was another sound of footsteps, these much closer by. With a rattle, the endless lift from the tower room below came to life. The trio watched in silent fear as the rungs came up and over and down the track. And then the helmet of a guard emerged from the hole in the floor. He twisted about to see whom he had been sent to find and, seeing them, almost but not quite, smiled. As soon as he could he stepped from the lift onto the floor beside them, and saluted Varina.

"Cian, you and your companions are requested to appear before the t'kyna to explain your presence here. Please follow me."

Five

As THE CHILDREN and Varina were ushered into the green room, they found a transparent wall had been built across one end of it, turning their space into an anteroom. Lights were focused on the wall in such a way that images were reflected as in a mirror, allowing only a dim view of the big figures moving on the other side of the glass.

The escorting guard pointed to the sofa, indicated they were to sit, and, when they had done so, retired to stand at ease by the double doors.

Silent minutes passed. Varina sat very still, eyes downcast, arms folded, waiting for whatever would come. The other two tried alternately to peer through the glass and to wait as patiently as she did. Finally Jason could stand the silence no longer. "I wish we could see what was going on," he whispered.

From the other side of the lucite panel came a sound like none he or Alta had ever heard before. It was like singing, but in tones so low and resonant the lucite shivered with vibration. Alta would have bolted had Varina not pulled her back onto the cushions. There was an answering note, higher than the first and more sibilant, and then the first singer resumed.

"What is that sound?" Jason whispered. "Are they talking?"

Varina nodded. "On their world the air is dense. Sound carries much as it does in water. When the winds are still . . ."—she paused—"Delikon sing as your extinct whales sang."

A whisper of static and a hidden wall speaker came on. An automatic translator activated, and over the singing sound the mechanical voice, pure of all inflection and emotion, asked, "You wished to see us?"

Jason, startled, blurted, "Yes," but his voice lacked conviction.

"Historically, sight of us proved traumatic to all your tribes. . . ." There was a pause, as if the speaker were mentally debating something. "No terrestrial now alive has seen us."

"Are their faces very ugly?" Alta whispered to Varina.

"No. They are beautiful, *I* think. But you will find them . . . very different."

Alta accepted this with a trusting nod. "Very well. If you think they're beautiful, I won't be afraid any more." But she took Varina's hand just in case.

The lights in the receiving area went off; the wall became transparent, and, for the first time in centuries, the Delikon let themselves be seen again by humankind.

"Oh my!" Alta breathed a sigh of awe. Inside were more than fifty "visitors"—and they were beautiful, but beautiful like nothing within human experience.

18

In the protective atmosphere of the room, they had removed their bubble helmets, and the indirect lighting gleamed off skin that appeared not skinlike but almost chitinous in texture. The cinnamon eyes were large, bright, and obliquely set to form the arms of a Y. The base of the Y gave the impression of nose and mouth. Jaw and cheekbones planed elegantly upward toward the earline—if those gleaming round membranes were sound sensors. With their brilliant capes close beneath their chins, it was difficult to see if they had necks. Their waists appeared to move like ball joints dividing torsos so heavily muscled that they looked segmented and mounted on long legs terminating in sturdy clawed "feet."

"Look at the hands," Jason blurted impulsively. Polished crystals sparkled from hands that had seven fingers, each tipped with a curious pad.

The Delikon nearest to them closed his eyes with deliberate slowness. Upper and lower lids met in the middle; the head became an ovoid with a cleft in the center.

"As we look alien to you, so your kind first appeared to us," the speaker advised. "The survival of your lifeform on a planet so inhospitable is most remarkable—frail, incomplete, your skin of little protection against your star's radiation, tiny eyes, and mouths like valves. Of all the creatures on your planet, your species most needed fur or feathers or scales. Had lifeform supremacy been based on beauty or strength, the tiger might have ruled earth. But we learned to appreciate the adaptive functionalism of your anatomic design, as you would appreciate ours could you see us on our home planet. The star that gives life to D'laak is large and distant, its light more gentle than earth's. Our world is twice the size of yours, our atmosphere dense and warm. Our lifeforms are as diverse as earth's once were—and you would find them as strange as your kind finds us—but no stranger than we found man or the giraffe. And we had seen lifeforms on many other worlds before yours."

Jason looked up at Varina for reassurance. He wasn't sure, but he suspected he was being rebuffed for his remark about the hands. With a slight nod of her head toward the visitors, she indicated he should pay attention to them only. But when he looked at the Delikon again, it had moved away from the barrier and stood near Sidra and Vashlin.

These two, along with other members of Kelador's Ruling House, wore bubble helmets in this atmosphere provided for their guests. There was a melodic rumbling, and then Sidra's voice was heard.

"You may return to your apartment and have your breakfast, children. You will mention this interview to no one. You will please remain, Varina."

Alta and Jason hesitated, their worry about what might happen to Varina clear on their faces. But the guard at the door had snapped to attention, and Varina whispered, "Go." They were escorted into the vestibule, and the big doors closed solidly behind them. Varina waited to hear Sidra's request for an explanation of her unorthodox behavior—for which Varina had no answer that would be acceptable. Sidra said nothing.

Instead the tallest and most gloriously caped of the Delikon approached now and closed its eyes in solemn salute. Varina rose and responded. When the Delikon spoke to her alone there was no translator; it used the songlike language of home. And what it told her was more frightening to her than any rebuke.

"You who endure the earth name of stranger, you who are young in our world and time, we salute you, Varina. You who endured with courage the parting, the journey, metamorphosis, exile, and pain, we praise you, Varina. To you will be given a name great with honor, a House blessed with riches and drones of your own. To you will be given long life and great power. We thank you, Varina."

From its hand the Delikon ambassador removed a

massive emerald ring and gave it to a subordinate to place into a wall recepticle. A panel slid shut on their side of the lucite and after a moment reopened onto the anteroom.

"Put on the ring," came the command.

Varina did so, over her hand to circle her wrist. The gem was space-grown, deep green and flawless as no earth crystal could ever be. On its table was carved the Seal of Privilege.

She looked at it gleaming in the dim light of the anteroom and knew its meaning. To those who wore these rings, and they were few, all Delikon paid tribute. But, more than that, it meant she could no longer put off facing the truth; she was to return. And suddenly she was very, very much afraid.

The ambassador had called her brave, she thought, but he did not know that the bravest act in her life was to continue to stand here now and observe the necessary protocol. When the Delikon were honored above all words, they wisely said nothing. And since her human form would have made ludicrous the Delikon gesture of gratitude, she instead clasped her hands together and bowed, which was a human custom, one she felt comfortable with.

Behind the ambassador, the other Delikon sounded the formal notes of praise, and, could those notes have been translated, they would have said, "Hail to Varina; praise her with great praise." To the others she also bowed. And they, in amused courtesy, recognizing her inability to respond properly with this body, bowed in return.

"You may go to my office chamber," Sidra said, rising now. "Wait for me there."

Had a guard not escorted her down the echoing hall to the other wing, Varina might have bolted. She did not know why she was so afraid; she was unaccustomed to fear. It was illogical and disorienting. She could feel the weight of the ring she wore on her wrist, the metal still cool from the ambassador's body. Until she had put it on she could pretend nothing was going to change—that she could stay here. But of course that was not true. The ring was "true," both in its privilege and in the responsibility that went with such privilege.

When Sidra entered her office she found Varina standing by the window that overlooked the reflecting pools.

"Why did you do it? Why did you jeopardize your record and their lives?"

"I wanted to see what they would think of . . . me . . . if I looked like that"—her disappointment at their initial reaction showed—". . . if they knew me as I really am. . . ."

Sidra's eyes widened at this all-too-human response. "You expected them not to be afraid? You are afraid of the tigers. As I am. Tigers are large animals—and we know they are dangerous. Consider how large a Delikon is to a human child . . ." She paused as another thought occurred. "Do you think they made or will make any connection between us and the Delikon? Or have you educated them on that subject also?"

"No!" said Varina. "I only said they were visitors from another part of the galaxy, that they came here in secret sometimes."

"And they believed you?"

"I have never lied to them before. I swore them to secrecy. They will never tell."

"And if they did they would be laughed at," concluded Sidra, and her voice softened as she observed, "You look as if you would like to indulge in the human custom of tears. No other member of earth's colonial administration has been awarded a Ring of Privilege. And you stand here grief-stricken."

"I am sorry," apologized Varina. "I do. . . ."

"No. *I* am sorry," interrupted Sidra, "for not forcing them to have you recalled long ago. Today is more our fault than yours. Not that that excuses your foolishness. But at your age, the chemical codings of habit are everything. Even to threaten disruption of that

22

bonding must produce confusion and fears I cannot imagine. It would perhaps be kind were I to have you anesthetized now. But I cannot. You have two final tasks to perform. You must take your companions to the sacred caves and advise them that they are ready for the academy. It could, of course, be done by a surrogate, but that would be traumatic to the children. Especially now. Can you do this?"

"Yes," said Varina, turning to catch Sidra watching her speculatively. Something in that look made her repeat, "Yes! I do not want someone else to tell them." Sidra, her eyes never blinking, stretched out on the chaise longue and continued to regard her. "I can do it," Varina insisted.

Sidra was distracted by a spot of dust on her elegant brown boots. "I know you can," she said, reaching down to remove the offending dust. "I was wondering if it was wise, knowing how you feel just now . . . you were to leave for the caves this morning. You never disobeyed a general order before. It shocked me when Bader said you were spying. I had not realized how disturbed all this made you. Suppose they had become hysterical—but then your companions never do. . . ." She paused as if still debating something, then changed her mind. "You have seven days left here and then your colonial service is ended. You have much to do. I will keep you no longer."

"It seems such a short time," said Varina wistfully, "seven days."

"All time seems short when something we enjoy is ending." Sidra stretched out her arm. "Come, take my hand. . . ."

"Will I see you again—here?" The thought that she might have to leave without saying good-bye upset her.

Sidra smiled. "You do plan to return from the mountains? Of course, I will see you." But then she did something highly unusual for a Delikon. She rose and embraced the child almost as a human might have done, and then, as if embarrassed by the gesture, she

23

hurried from the room. Varina stood in pleased confusion and noticed only minutes later that she ached from the force of that hug. And somehow it had removed the worst of the fear.

Six

WHEN THE MOUNTAINS obscured further view of the convoy, the solitary rider let his horse pick its careful way down the ridge to the timberline. There, in a grove of mountain ash, a small band of riders waited. They waved as he rode up, looking like an unkempt guide reporting to senior officers. He returned the salute, but he was not glad to see them. Unlike them, he was trespassing in Kelador. Like them, he had once belonged here.

His name was Aron then. It was the name the Delikon gave him when he was two. Like all chosen children, he never knew his real name or where he had come from. Kelador was his home through the long years of childhood, Kelador's boundary the limit of all he knew and cared about. He crossed that boundary at the age of twelve. He had never returned until today.

"You saw the machines?" one of the riders asked.

"I saw them."

The others waited for him to elaborate, and, when he did not, one said, "Well, is it military equipment?"

"No."

"How can you be sure?" said another.

For the first time since he had joined them, Aron seemed to give them his full attention. "Use common sense. Do you honestly think that if Kelador even suspected our plans, any of us would be alive—let alone within her borders, or guests at the sanctuary?"

"We're taking quite a risk just meeting you here. . . ."

"You are taking no more of a risk than you have ever taken, governor," Aron said bluntly.

"We formulated the strategy to end Kelador's tyranny," a woman reminded him.

"Agreed," Aron said, "and you appointed me commander for three reasons—namely, my sector offers the best point of attack; my people are the poorest and most desperate, and last but hardly least, I am the only leader among us whom you all trust."

"You have the most to gain," said a woman with steel-blue hair and a voice to match.

"And the most to lose, Julia," he said gently. "I lost more than a thousand people tunneling beneath and taking the first tower."

"You were attacked?" There was a murmur of alarm.

He shook his head. "Not by people. By our own poor equipment. And ignorance. Automatic lasers guard not only the border but every tunnel, every room. We learned their location and range the hard way. Have you ever seen a man lasered? Ever smelled . . . ?"

"Don't be vulgar," Julia said quickly. "We have incurred losses of our own taking over the transmitting stations in our sectors. It gave our people more incentive. . . ."

One of the horses whinnied with impatience; another answered, and they all shifted restlessly.

"The horses have no patience with rhetoric either," said Aron. "We shouldn't spend so much time in one place. Come. We can talk as we ride. What I want to know from you is how quickly you can move your armies, such as they are, once we breach the boundary. Can I count on you?"

He led them back through the hills, along narrow valleys and trails unused since he had explored them as a boy. Even as his cohorts talked, he wished he were alone to savor the melancholy pleasure of seeing old haunts. By midmorning they had reached a well-worn bridle path. Then six rode east. Aron alone rode west.

As he rode he tried to visualize this trail as it might look after an army had passed along it. The thought of its ruin deepened his mood of depression.

Revolution was all very well in theory. The people's cause was just. Kelador was a tyranny—ruthless, oppressive in its adherence to strict conformity to caste, to laws without human logic, demanding the best and leaving only enough. Never more. The whispered demand for equality grew louder with each generation. He himself had whispered with the loudest.

But after these past three months he was silent. Now that war was almost inevitable, he was no longer sure it was wise. But perhaps he was wrong. He had always been taught, always believed, the people of Kelador to be a superior race. He was as sure of that as he was of his own elite caste—until lately. And he suspected that members of the upper caste believed themselves superior to those in lower castes, if for no other reason than that they had always been taught to believe it. Who would define equality? Who would accept it—if it meant a loss of status?

The doubts began the day they destroyed one of the Keladorian bases and he had ordered what he thought was a storage arsenal blasted open. The building had been a vacuum container. Six of his people were killed in the implosion. The building had contained not armaments but the remains of creatures whose bodies had been powdered by the blast. It was impossible to tell what they might have been. There was no one outside Kelador with that kind of education. But the creatures were not of earth, not of an earth Aron ever knew. Of that he was positive—almost.

Aron was intelligent enough to guess that in spite of his ten years as a companion, his ignorance about

26

the Ruling House was limitless. On the basis of intuition alone he had ordered all power shut off to all Keladorian arsenals. On the logical level, he could not explain why, not without appearing to have gone insane. After he admitted those first doubts, the others came crowding in. Suppose the revolution failed? Would there be inhuman retribution? As in the old myths . . . if they were myths. And if the revolution succeeded, would the new government be more humane? Or merely human?

If the people of Kelador were not human . . . but that he found almost impossible to believe. Varina had been the most human person he had ever known. "And you never found another person like her, did you?" an irritated Julia had once said. "She was perfection, an angel, in your mind." Lately he had begun to wonder if Julia had been more right than she knew. Or did Julia suspect too?

Why didn't the Keladorians age?

Because he had learned that self-doubt was more destructive than the most formidable enemy, he stopped thinking. Instead he concentrated on the songs of birds in the trees around him. Once he had known each bird by its song. He listened to the rhythmic creaking of his saddle, watched the wind gusts part the horse's black mane, felt his thigh muscles burn and ache from his too-long ride. And he considered how old he felt and how good it was to be alone in the mountains on a beautiful day.

It was midafternoon when he rode out of the old tunnel onto his side of the boundary. An hour later his aircar met him.

"Do you want to return to headquarters or to camp, sir?" The pilot's voice interrupted his thoughts.

"The camp, please. No . . . where is the road construction crew now? We'll go there first before I forget."

As he sank into the soft leather seat, it occurred to him that it was the comfort and convenience that accompanied power that made power itself so seductive. Varina had never taught him that. Perhaps she had always taken it for granted, knowing nothing else. Perhaps she had been ignorant too.

Seven

THE CAVES OF COSMIC ORDER were located above the timberline in a remote part of the mountains. For eight months of the year snow blocked all access to them. Sheer cliffs allowed no place for aircraft to land. The only approach was a twisting narrow trail wide enough to permit horsemen to ride single file.

Designed as a data source for the interstellar races who might follow, the caves were in essence a vast museum, containing in indestructible replication the results of aeons of earth's evolution. Man and his works occupied a limited space. The caves were a shrine not for man but for the Delikon.

At the entrance to the caves stood the sanctuary. Here lived the human artisans and caretakers, many of them people who by their devotion to the abstract had escaped their caste and became here truly religious. Here also, at intervals, lived members of the Ruling House who came to supervise or make their own contribution, or simply contemplate the infinite patience of the Creators.

Because Sidra had wanted the palace cleared before the ambassadors arrived, Varina, Alta, and Jason were to have left at five that morning to visit the caves. Varina's escort, Cornelius, had flown on ahead the evening before to the village in the foothills where the trail to the caves began. He had taken all their luggage with him. Since part of the trip was by horseback, and the children always packed unessentials, Cornelius found it prudent to make up the packhorse's

28

load in private. The children were to join him at seven the next morning.

As befits a personal bodyguard, for that is what he was, Cornelius was large. He looked like an aging warrior, going gray, with great veins beginning to cord over the muscles on his brown arms. He was soft-spoken and as gentle as a big dog that has no enemies to fear.

When their aircar landed in early afternoon he was waiting for them. Four saddle horses and a pack horse were also waiting in the shade at the edge of the landing pad. The horses looked far more at ease than the man. He greeted them with the irritation that follows hours of worry.

He did not ask her why he had been kept waiting; pride prevented that, and she could not tell him. With Varina feeling guilty, Cornelius irked, and Alta and Jason lost in some glum mood of their own, it was a very quiet uphill ride through the woods.

From several miles down the mountain, the riders heard the sanctuary carillons heralding their approach. The clear notes struck the air to echo and re-echo in the distance, and Varina felt the peace in them still some of the turmoil in her mind.

"Where are the bells coming from?" said Alta. "I can't see anything." The ravine through which the trail led was a narrow slit between two walls of red limestone.

"We are near the sanctuary. Sensors in the cliff warn of visitors and activate the carillon."

"Why do they want to be warned?" asked Jason. "What are they afraid of?"

"Nothing," Cornelius answered. "They are afraid of nothing." It was the first time he had spoken since they set out.

Varina looked at him and wondered. This trip was nothing new for him. He had been her servant for more than thirty years and had seen three previous sets of companions grow up and leave. She knew he suspected, although he was not sure, that other pairs had preceded those.

Cornelius was one of those humans who held Varina and her kind in awe. But he did not fear them. He had never had cause to. At twenty-five, he had viewed her as a too-intelligent kid sister. At thirty, he admired her. By the time he was fifty, his wife had died and his children were grown and busy with their own lives, but Varina remained the one constant thing in his existence. Like a dream one retreats to when reality presses, she never changed, and he loved her for that above all.

Varina could and did empathize with her companions because, like them, she was a child far from her birthplace, molded by others to serve a purpose. But empathy was more emotion than logic and it occurred to her as she considered Cornelius that she really knew very little about adult humans, except that they had always been kind to her—especially this one.

If she was going to return with the ambassadors' ship, he would have to be told she was leaving; be given some excuse for her total departure from his life. She dreaded a last meeting with him far more than saying good-by to Alta and Jason. They would miss her, but they loved her out of need, as all human children loved, as they would love the next person who cared for them. But she sensed that her absence would leave a permanent gap in Cornelius's life now, and there was no way she could change that. After all this time she couldn't even tell him the truth. Instead she would tell him what Sidra and policy dictated, some well-intentioned lie. As she considered the pain that lie might inflict on the man, she suddenly remembered Sidra saying, "I no longer allow myself the luxury of loving any other than my own kind," and understood why.

All the way up the mountain the steel shoes of the horses had clanked against the stone. Now, as they rounded a corner, it was as if the horses had stepped onto moss. Directly ahead, the trail ended in a box canyon. Varina reined up, dismounted, and walked to the wall. After searching a moment, she pressed both palms against a shiny spot on the stone. What had at first glance appeared to be natural fracturing lines suddenly began to split and the gate to the sanctuary opened.

Inside was a graveled oblong of courtyard bordered by emerald grass and ornate landscaping. Warm flower-scented air floated out, carrying with it the warble of songbirds.

Varina didn't bother to remount but led her horse through the gate as her guests and servant followed. The gate shut behind them. The bells could no longer be heard. It was as if they had entered a very large solarium.

To their right trees and vines softened and shielded the stone wall that stretched to the stables. A fountain jetted in the middle of the avenue. To the left a wide sweep of flagstone steps fluted down from the ivy-draped granite of the sanctuary. Coming down the steps was a welcoming delegation in flowing robes of muted color.

"We welcome you, cian." The white-haired man who led the little group bowed to her. "It always gives us pleasure to anticipate your visits and satisfaction to see you once again."

"It is good to see you again, keeper," she said. And it was. She had known this keeper since his infancy—as she had known his parents and grandparents. "I bring Alta and Jason to view the caves—and Cornelius because he refused to stay home."

The white-haired man bowed gravely to the young future governors and then, as the old friend he was, smiled and clasped Cornelius's hands. "You will have dinner with us, of course," he said, and Cornelius accepted the invitation.

The children dined that evening in a room where wood paneling and green carpet made the space an extension of the gardens directly beyond the windows.

Fine paintings adorned the walls; crystal and goldware sparkled on linen.

There were other diners—elderly men and women, administrators who had succeeded in regaining entry to Kelador, scholars from the academies, philosophers. They wore the formal evening garb of their sector, and the pastel uniforms glowed in the soft lighting. There was a murmur of conversation that came to a sudden halt when the children entered.

Varina had expected the silence; it always happened in places where people seldom saw members of the Ruling House. On her first visit it had embarrassed her, the way they stared at her uniform and more discreetly at her eyes. She suspected that but for their rank a few would have whispered as the distant villagers whispered, "She's one of them!" She told herself she had become used to the stares, but she never did. Nor was she flattered by them.

As always, some diners looked at her as if they thought they should know her but couldn't quite remember her name. Some of them seemed familiar too, but she could not remember their childhood names, and she was never told the names they later assumed. Those who returned to Kelador seldom did so until they were past middle age. By that time gravity had molded their faces beyond her recognition . . . and in their memories her face had long since subtly altered to suit their own inner vision.

It seemed to her that it took longer than usual for the chatter to resume tonight; the watchful quiet was almost hostile. While she had expected the hush, its effect on Alta and Jason was unnerving.

"I'm sorry," said Alta to an old man at a nearby table who was staring at her. "Did we interrupt something?"

"No, child." He was instantly gracious. "Forgive us, I think we all had forgotten how young we once were. Enjoy your meal!" He gave her a smile of dismissal and then began speaking to the man across from him. As if at a signal, normal sounds returned to the room.

"What was that all about?" asked Jason, and then his attention was distracted by a servant hurrying past with a loaded tray. "Chicken and noodles with buttered croutons," he announced. "Let's order. I'm starving!"

For as many people as occupied it, the room was very quiet, as if the adults were absorbed in some private preoccupation.

"Can we talk?" whispered Alta after their order was taken.

"Of course, but softly," said Varina.

"How come no one else is?"

"They are, but . . ."

"I know, softly." Alta made a face. "It's like eating in a temple."

Varina grinned. "It is not that bad." She deliberately spoke in normal tones. "They come here to meditate. Being very quiet becomes habit." Then she changed the subject and in a little while Alta and Jason were at ease again.

But she was not. In spite of herself she found she was analyzing what was different about this group tonight. She remembered the people here looking serene; these looked tense and anxious. Why did no one come over to their table to meet Alta and Jason and congratulate them on achieving this goal? It was common courtesy here and had always been done—before. Instead she caught several almost pitying glances in their direction, and a subtle shade of contempt when they met her eyes. Or was she imagining it all?

Eight

TO REACH THE CAVES one followed a mossy flagstone path through the garden, past the stables, and up a wide curve of steps to where a gatekeeper stood, dwarfed by the massive doors behind him.

33

The doors were a glazed blue so brilliant that, had they not been shaded from the sun, they would have pained human eyes. In deep-set inlays of gold, in what at first glance seemed to be mere decorative pattern, were a series of spirals, circles, and straight lines. In one tiny equiangular spiral on the left door two jewels glistened, a sapphire halfway from its center, an emerald above and to the right.

"Does that mean anything?" Jason pointed to the design.

"It is a map, very stylized. And a code system . . ." Varina hesitated, then changed the subject. "Notice how the doors are angled into the side of the cliff? Sometime this greenhouse roof will be gone and then the gate will be visible from the air. . . ."

The gatekeeper bowed to them. "Welcome to the Spiral Caves of Cosmic Order. Do you wish to enter?"

Varina said they did.

"Please exchange your boots for slippers to protect the floor." From an alcove he provided black velvet slippers, and when they had put them on, he told them, "The companions will sign the guest book."

After she had written her name, Alta flipped back through the pages to look at the signatures. Many were famous, known even to her from textbooks or video association. But a half-inch thickness covered a century. "Not many people get to come here, do they?" she said, smiling up into the gatekeeper's cinnamon eyes.

"Only the favored ones," he said soberly and turned to Varina. "The galleries are empty for you, cian. Shall I come for you at the end of the lesson? Or do you remember the path?"

"I remember."

"Very well." He replaced the book and pressed a silent switch that caused the doors to swing inward onto darkness.

"Come," said Varina and they followed her in.

She had always hated the caves. From the very first time she came here, the sound of those massive doors closing behind her had caused her near panic. The fear grew with each trip. She was closed within the earth, behind rock, with uncalculated tons of rock above, at the mercy of circuitry for light, air, and eventual release. This was one place where logic held no soothing magic for her. No matter how often she told herself, "You are safe," she *knew* she was not—because she always remembered that when the proper time came, a switch would be thrown that sealed this whole enormous complex and vacuumized it in darkness until the day the code on the door would be read and understood and the door reopened to a new race of conquerors.

"How beautiful," breathed Alta.

And it was.

They stood beneath a great dome of fused white granite gold-flecked with mica. Suspended from the high ceiling by an invisible support hung what appeared to be a greatly enlarged cross-section of a chambered nautilus, illuminated by a green key light. Along the left side of the vaulting space ran an arched colonnade off of which brightly lit galleries wound. Repeated above the various gallery entrances were the same symbols that marked the great outer door.

Because this place intimidated her, as it always had, Varina became more lecturer than friend. "You will note the perfection achieved by time and space—a spiral produced by a combination of rotation and expansion; a growing, ordered geometric progression, ever expanding. So is and so shall be your comprehension."

Alta and Jason exchanged glances and a smile escaped, first on her face, and spread to his. Varina stopped in mid-lecture. "What is it?"

"You!" giggled Alta. "You sound like a text. Couldn't you just walk with us through the halls and let us look? I think we'd all enjoy it more."

"And if we have questions, we'll ask," added Jason.

"But you do not yet know enough to ask!"

"Then how can we understand what you tell us?"

35

"Because I will tell it simply," insisted Varina. "This is our final lesson. The earth was born of cosmic dust. You were born of earth; you are a product of its oceans. In the spirals of your chromosomes are the codes, repeated since life began on your planet, which link you to all life. And each of your cells has its ocean counterpart swimming there still. The earth's minerals, chemicals, gases, liquids are in those single cells—all cooperating for life. All compose the creature that is you. As the circling planets compose the solar systems; as the solar systems compose our spiral galaxy; as the galaxies compose the infinite spiral of the universe. You are one creature. So is the universe one creature, and we are each a cell within its structure. We are part of the cosmic order. The caves illustrate the beauty and perfection of cosmic order, its infinite discipline, and its ultimate purpose."

She searched their faces, trying to judge if they understood. Both looked a bit blank. Then finally Alta asked, "Is that all true, or is it your religion?"

"She means, is it a philosophy?" Jason said, not wanting to offend.

"Not philosophy, but a form of truth," said Varina.

"It makes me feel about as important as a grain of wheat," said Alta.

"Oh, but it should reassure you," Varina said quickly. "We each of us have our place in life, our assigned function to perform." But as she spoke she realized that she had quit thinking about it long ago; it made her feel as the caves made her feel, insignificant and in danger of being trapped. But that was heresy.

"Can we see the galleries?" said Jason. "Maybe it will be clearer to me then."

For hours she walked with them through this display of Delikon ingenuity, this alien tribute to the wealth of diversity that was earth in all its phases of evolution, both inanimate and animate. For Varina the most fascinating galleries were those of the single-celled creatures. Enlarged hundreds, sometimes thousands of times, exactly detailed and pulsating with pseudolife, these models of diatoms, mold spores, bacteria, egg cells, and the like, were as breathtaking in their perfection as snowflakes. Like all her companions, Alta and Jason pronounced them interesting and "pretty," but what they truly enjoyed were the displays devoted to their own species. They went through all those galleries twice.

There was one corridor in this section which they could not enter; the way was barred by a green door on which was engraved a legend in script totally foreign to them. And if Varina knew what was displayed behind that door, she did not say.

From one chamber to the next they wandered, at first marveling, then slowly becoming overwhelmed by both the immensity and the implied meaning of the place. The more they saw, the less clear it all became, like the eye of a needle seen at one-million magnification.

At last they reached a small circular chamber in the innermost spiral. In its center stood a round pillar. Varina pressed something and a door in the pillar slid open. "This leads to the last exhibit," she said. "It is quite special."

The elevator had a faint odor of cave, damp moss, and lichen although it was carpeted and brightly lit. The ride down lasted several minutes, until the elevator door opened onto a bare cold tunnel. "Are we going to like this?" asked Jason.

"You will never forget it," Varina assured him.

The white tunnel ended at a round blue door, and, as they approached, the door halved and slid open onto darkness. Had Varina not walked on, the other two would have frozen with fear on the threshold. She appeared to have stepped out into space—a space enormous, vast, and deep. Infinite. She looked back and, seeing their fear, took their hands and led them into the emptiness. The door closed silently behind them.

Their feet made no sound on the transparent floor. Beneath that floor, overhead and all around them stretched the Milky Way. Against the blackness of space planets silently circled stars, and the stars were beyond count. It was beauty on a scale almost beyond human acceptance, for no matter how long one looked, it could never be fully seen, fully comprehended. Only specifics could be absorbed; the small red dwarf that burned beyond an icy blue giant, the wine pansy-bloom of a nebula whose gaseous petals must billow a million miles and whose center would form a sun to dwarf their own; the minute streaks of light that were comets, cosmic debris.

Varina stopped to let them drink in the wonder. When it seemed to her they had been sufficiently awed, she led them by an unmarked path to a point of the floor where directly below nine small planets circled one small star. It took them time in their awestruck state to recognize their own solar system, tiny as it was in this scaled model, and then they knelt to better watch the fragile blue earth with its minute moon silently circle the tiny flaming sun.

Varina's voice was hushed. "Earth is one small planet of one small star in one small galaxy. Yet small as our galaxy seems to be here"—with a wave of her arm she included all the vastness around—"it takes light one hundred thousand earth years to cross it. Within this galaxy we have found one hundred ninety populated planets. There may be a million more. And all this is only a minute portion of the Creature called Universe, that consists of one hundred billion galaxies."

"Are they *all* here?" whispered Alta, and Varina laughed.

"No, no. This is only the Milky Way. The finest miniaturists of any world could not make a scale model of Universe—not if they worked forever. Nor could we endure the endless reality of seeing it, could it be done. For our perception is mercifully limited where matter and time are involved. But by seeing the parts we can dimly perceive the Whole."

"Does this, all this, form a spiral?" Alta was guessing, but Varina's pleased smile told her the guess was correct.

"And the other galaxies—do they spiral?" said Jason.

"Some of them . . ."

"Is this what we are to understand?"

"Part of it."

"And the rest?"

"Will come with age and meditation."

"I don't think I'm going to like it when I know," said Alta. "If those people in the dining room were happy . . ."

"I don't want to be that happy," concluded Jason.

They wandered the galaxy, Varina talking, explaining, the other two listening, following. Jason and Alta had no idea where they were. The path Varina followed included both up and down ramps; star systems which at one point were at eye level for them appeared again far overhead or off at a tangent below, which was confusing until they realized that there were many levels and what was floor was also ceiling. But there seemed to be no walls, no beginning and no end.

"Now I understand what people mean when they say 'lost in space,' " said Alta at last. "How do we get out of here?"

"We don't," said Jason. "We orbit endlessly and never get home for supper."

"That's not funny, Jason!" She turned to Varina. "It's all very beautiful and very interesting but—well, besides being hungry—I just want to get out. Can we, please?"

Varina hesitated. Not because she didn't want to leave, but because she had not wanted to come here to begin with and guilt made her feel she should be especially thorough. If they could only begin to see the corollary now between one life form and all life forms, between one world and all worlds. But her friends' eyes were dazed with fatigue.

"Cian . . . cian Varina." The gatekeeper's voice

boomed around them like the voice of God. "Cian Varina?"

"Yes?"

"Is all well with you and your guests?"

"Yes. Why do you intrude?"

"I beg your pardon, cian, but it is long past the dinner hour and the keeper wished assurance of your safety."

"Thank you. We are on level nine. We are coming up."

"I will send the elevator," boomed the voice. A moment later a faint bell rang and an oblong of light appeared ahead of them. Jason gave an unconscious sigh of relief.

"Why did he ask if we were safe? Do many people get lost down here?"

"No. But some go mad," Varina said bluntly. "Come." And she set off toward the warmth of that blessed human oblong of light with the other two almost treading her heels in their hurry to reach it. Had it been possible to pass her without colliding with stars, they would have done so.

Nine

TIRED THOUGH SHE WAS, Varina could not fall asleep. Outside, a cold wind blustered and made spasmodic attempts to shake the building. Inside all was warm and still, except within her troubled mind. She lay with her hands clasped behind her head, stared wide-eyed up at the stars, and wondered which one of those lights was the Delikon ship.

She had considered running away, getting lost in the mountains. If she could hide for ten days, the ship would leave without her. But Cornelius would never let her get lost. Or if she did, he would find her.

Should he fail to find her, he would suffer for her act. And that would never do. She would have to return to the palace. Which meant that within five days her restructuring would begin. In ten days she would be up there, aboard the starship, looking out one of its windows, wondering which tiny light below was earth. And she was afraid.

With no warning knock her bedroom door opened stealthily. Two dark figures entered and moved toward her bed. Covers rustled as she reached for the light.

"Don't," whispered Jason. "You'll blind us. Why are you awake? Can you see the flashes, too?"

"What flashes?"

"Come to my room; the view's best there." Alta had knelt and was patting the floor. "Where are your slippers? These tile floors are cold."

In Alta's room the windows faced west and a whole new set of stars could be seen, but not much else. "Just wait," they told her. "Keep watching." She would not have noticed the first light except that distant snow peaks momentarily became visible against the horizon. Then came a second flare.

"Heat lightning?"

"Too cold. Too dry."

"Maybe aurora borealis?"

"Not high enough. It seems to be coming from the surface. Some of the beams flare straight up."

"We were wondering," whispered Alta, "maybe it has something to do with those big . . . ambassadors who came?"

"Never," Varina said quickly. "No. They never call attention to themselves."

There came a final flash that paled the night, lit the snow on the mountain tops, and glared off the veralite dome below. All three instinctively jumped away from the window. A great gust of wind rushed against the building so fast and hard that slates on the roof snapped loose and came rattling down to shatter on the greenhouse dome.

"Wow! Something blew up!"

"But what?" wondered Varina.

"Why don't we go see tomorrow?" suggested Jason. "You said we had at least a day to go camping if we wanted to. Why don't we go exploring?"

"Let's ask her the other thing, too?" Alta had the tone of someone who had decided to get the worst over with first before considering pleasure.

"Okay." Jason sighed. "You ask her."

"Ask me what?" Varina was imagining all sorts of awkward questions regarding the Delikon, and when Alta said, "Are we going to the academy soon?" out of sheer surprise she simply said, "Yes. When we get back. How did you know?"

"Well, we're not stupid!" Alta sounded a little miffed. "I mean, we've always known. . . . Otherwise we wouldn't be living in the palace and you wouldn't be our teacher. And it had to come sometime. We are almost as old as you are."

Varina was glad the darkness hid her smile.

"Besides, you kept saying things like this being our last lesson. And looking at us like you were never going to see us again. And the things the keeper said when we got here . . ." Jason sat down with a disgruntled thump on the bed and folded his legs beneath him. "I know it's a great honor to be chosen—and we'll probably really like it when we get used to it . . ."

"But at the moment you would rather not go?" said Varina. "I know the feeling. I should have told you about this before. I have known for weeks that you were to leave soon for the academy. But it seemed a shame to spoil each good time with the thought that it might be The Last Time."

"It's because the meteor came," Alta said mournfully. "The gardener was right; meteors are bad omens. Look what followed this one. Monsters and—"

"Don't be silly!" Varina was stung by that word "monster." "You have always known about the academy. It has nothing to do with omens. I have taught you as much as I can. It is unfair to keep you here any longer."

"But it would be nice," Jason said wistfully. "Just for another year, Varina? Please?"

She shook her head. "No. That cannot be." She was almost pleading. "We have talked about the academy for years. You have always wanted to go."

"Yes," admitted Alta. "But talk is different from the real thing. Why do we have to go away? Why can't they move the academy here?"

"Because going away is good for you. You must learn what change is or your mind will not expand. You must meet new people, see new places, learn specific things. By the time you serve your apprenticeships you will understand how to design and build houses and dams and roads; know your sector's growing cycle, its crops, resources, transport systems; learn everything from law to economics to the water table at specific times of the year; learn all the things that affect your people and your world . . ."

"That sounds like a lot," said Jason.

"You will have years in which to learn it," she assured him.

"I don't know if I can do that."

Varina thought for a moment and then asked, "What is the proportion of the golden mean?"

".618034 to 1," they both said in unison.

"What does it form?"

"An eight-note octave, a playing card, a sunflower . . ." Jason counted them off and was going on when Alta said, "A logarithmic spiral."

"Yes, but that's dull." Jason objected.

"The result of that ratio?" continued Varina.

"Stability of form," Alta said.

"And it's pleasing to see and hear," said Jason.

"You will never have to understand anything more difficult, or more simple, than that at the academy," Varina promised.

They thought this over for a while, and then Alta said, "We won't see you after this, will we? Once we leave the palace, that is?"

"No. But you know that too. It is one of the oldest laws."

She sensed in their silence the fears they were too polite to express. "It will be hard for you at first. You will miss me, miss the palace. But your homesickness will pass. You will make new friends, have new teachers." As she spoke she suddenly had a glimpse of how Sidra may have felt when reassuring her about going home and felt a surge of empathy for her guardian. "At any rate, wishing will change nothing. We all live by the laws of the Ruling House. So we may as well stop talking about it."

"Can I ask one more question?" said Alta. "What will you do when we go?"

"Miss you." Varina said lightly. "I shall miss you very much. And that too cannot be changed. Now I am going to call and leave a message for Cornelius, and then I am going to bed. If we have a long ride ahead of us tomorrow, we will all need our sleep."

Ten

ALTHOUGH IT WAS STILL DARK in the valleys, the sun was bright on the mountain top when they rode out early the next morning. The air outside the gate was crisp. It took them an hour to cover the most tortuous part of the trail. By that time both children and horses were impatient to run. As soon as the trail widened, Varina gave her mare a slap on its gleaming brown rump and galloped off with Alta and Jason in pursuit.

"You'll break your necks," Cornelius assured them cheerfully, knowing they would not. He followed at a more sedate pace with the pack horse in tow.

For today at least she was free, Varina thought as she rode. She had no more lessons to teach, no sched-

44

ule to follow, nothing that *had* to be done. And earth was such a pretty world! She began to sing. Behind her Alta and Jason joined in. The jolts of galloping that gave the singing a hiccuped effect made them all laugh. A stranger seeing them pass by with the wind in their hair, red suited and gold caped, mounted on fine horses, might have envied them their joy and what he imagined their lives to be.

They rode down the mountain, crossed a connecting slope, and then rode down again in lazy switchbacks. At the timberline their trail crossed a fork. The original trail went south toward the village where the monitor craft was to meet them the next day. The fork led southwest. They took the fork and rode for miles along a broad pass through the mountains.

Nowhere was there any evidence of storm damage from lightning or any other catastrophe. The valley had an almost primeval quality about it; huge beech and oaks mingled with old pines. The wildlife watched curiously as they rode by, but not even rabbits fled until Alta and Jason talked to them. Waterfalls flashed down from the ridges, white ribbons against the gray cliffs. Occasionally, where the soil was soft, they could see the tracks of a lone horseman who had ridden west ahead of them, but there was no other sign of human life.

Rest and lunch had come and gone. They were crossing an upland meadow, approaching the mountain sprawling across the western end of the pass.

"What's that hole ahead?" Alta called. "If it's a cave, can we explore it?"

"If it's safe," answered Cornelius.

"Why spoil the day by going into a cave?" Varina wanted to know.

As they rode closer, Varina saw that it was not a cave but a tunnel of human design. She turned to look back the way they had come and wondered if this pass had also been the work of man. When viewed with that thought, the fact that all the mountains ended in such conveniently sheer cliffs seemed more than na-

45

ture's handiwork. She was impressed, never having seen any of the engineering antiquities of earth. For aesthetic reasons all had been removed from Kelador.

The tunnel, bored around the mountain centuries before to speed surface traffic to one of the few unspoiled parts of the world, had windows cut from the rock to provide daylight and spectacular views. Over the centuries part of the rock walls had collapsed onto the tunnel floor. Stalactites dripped overhead. Inside each window trees and vines had taken root in the floor. But the tunnel was still passable by horse or on foot. They emerged from it twenty minutes later to find themselves on a cliff with no way down. They could turn around or go on. Immediately ahead was a second tunnel.

They entered it, and it seemed endless. From its windows one could see far across the mountains and down into the valley. Clouds drifted in lazy fluffs below them, casting moving patches of shade across the treetops. Occasionally, a cloud would brush against the side of their mountain and fog would pour through the windows, only to be driven out or dispersed by the cool air currents that swept along the curving passageway. When that happened Alta and Jason would yell with delight at being lost in the mist, and the horses would whicker and shy. The sounds of horses and humans echoed in the hollowness. Their smells mingled with far older scents of water and decaying stone impregnated with hydrocarbons.

Though the rest of the party was enjoying itself, Varina felt increasingly anxious, about what she did not know—perhaps the dimness and the ruin. When the discomfort became too great she reined up at a window, dismounted, and let her horse browse on the greenery. She leaned out and enjoyed the view that stretched for miles beyond and below. A flash of light caught her eye and she turned. It took almost ten seconds for the shock to register. On a mountain perhaps two miles away stood a tower, its rotating an-

46

tenna sparkling in the sun. While riding this ancient covered roadway, they had crossed the boundary!

Towers like this one marched across the peaks that encircled Kelador, guarding it, shutting out the rest of the world, keeping in those foolish enough to want to leave. It was common knowledge that powerful lasers in those towers covered each portion of the boundary. Those who crossed at unscheduled points were killed. The firing was automatic, activated by human body temperature. Upon firing, an alarm went off; in due time a patrol arrived at the target site to identify the victim. So she had always believed. But perhaps it was not true—or perhaps it was. She dropped to her knees and, with the protection of the rock wall behind her, grabbed her mare's reins and tugged her away from the danger.

"We crossed the boundary!" she called at full volume. The other three were out of sight around the bend ahead. "Keep away from the windows!"

"Windows! Windows! Windows!" came a mocking echo. A brick fell from the wall.

.."What?" Jason yelled. "What? What?" said the echo.

"We crossed the boundary!" she called again, and "boundary" echoed and re-echoed. She remounted and gave the mare a slap for speed just as Cornelius came galloping around the curve. He reached out and caught her reins.

"Are you all right? What's wrong?" He searched her face and body as if expecting to find her damaged. "Why did you cry out like that? I didn't know you could make such a sound!"

.."We crossed the boundary! The lasers—keep away from the windows . . . " She saw his expression change from worry to puzzlement.

Alta and Jason came cantering up. "What's the matter?"

"Stay here—all of you." And, ignoring Varina's protests, Cornelius dismounted and walked over to the window. With his back to the full wall, he extended his left hand out of the opening. All four of them held their breaths and waited. One minute passed, and they dared to breathe. Two, and Cornelius waved his full arm. No laser fired. He turned and looked out at the tower. When he walked back to the children, he moved as though drained of energy. Varina waited for him to speak. "It does look like a boundary tower," he said. "But it is not. I have seen them operate . . . before we even saw it was . . ." The man paused and met her eyes. "It must be a weather or transmission station of some type, cian. Otherwise you and I would definitely be dead."

She nodded, feeling foolish. He was right of course. If she were logical about being underground, she would not have overreacted like this. "I am so very sorry I frightened you, Cornelius. It did panic me."

He grinned up at her at that admission. "So few things do that I will mark this day in my diary as unique," he said as he remounted. "The tunnel ends ahead and we'll soon make camp. I think it's time."

The mouth of the tunnel glowed green and yellow with sunstruck leaves. Cornelius dismounted to hold the branches back so the children could ride past. The roadbed ended here, washed away by time, but the path was still visible. The forested slope below them curved with glacial smoothness around the next mountain. The retreating sun had already left the trees in shade.

They camped beside a snow brook that meandered through a grove of old pines. As always on camping trips, they had their own duties. Jason set up the tent; Varina and Alta took care of the horses, and Cornelius was the cook. By sunset the pine grove smelled of coffee and barbecuing steaks. The horses were eating and their riders ready to.

"Someone's coming," Cornelius said, and paused to listen, fork in hand. "Horsemen. Hear them?" Jason's curly head emerged from the tent. "Who's up here?" He sounded cross at their not having the mountains to themselves.

A group of riders appeared among the trees below. Only Varina could see them in detail at this distance; they looked very foreign to her. They were dressed in a mixture of common garb and shabby uniforms of unknown caste and rank. She walked away from the campfire to see more clearly, and, as she did so, one of them raised binoculars to his eyes and then almost immediately gave a command. The troop halted.

Varina watched the man with the binoculars, which were now focused on her, and she saw the look on his face change from frowning to fear. After studying her for a long moment he hurriedly scanned the other three, then redirected his attention to her. She could see the mouths of the riders beside him moving, apparently asking questions.

"What are they doing, cian?" Cornelius came across the clearing to stand beside her.

"Discussing us. I do not know what they are, Cornelius."

"I'll send them on their way," he said reassuringly. But he looked worried. The behavior of these strangers was odd. To sit and stare at uniforms of the Ruling House? "I wonder how long it's been since they were out of these hills for them to act like this . . . well, at least they're going to come up and say hello."

"The education office is failing somewhere," Varina agreed, and noted something else. The riders seemed to be carrying weapons, long riflelike affairs of crude design which they were withdrawing from saddle holsters as they approached.

They encircled the camp, some of them crossing the stream to do so, and then drew in closer.

Although courtesy demanded a commoner extend first greetings to a person of rank, these men and women said nothing. Interesting, Varina thought. I have never seen anything like them. They are not even clean.

The man with the binoculars muttered something to the woman beside him, and she shook her head.

"I know we're a long way from the palace, but it is

49

common courtesy to greet a teacher and her companions," Cornelius called to them.

At this the woman turned to another rider and Varina heard her say, "Teacher?" The man nodded and seemed to confirm it, but Varina could not understand his words.

"Maybe they're deaf?" said Alta.

"No . . ."—Varina didn't think so—"no . . . I think they do not understand the language . . ." and a forbidding chill swept over her. These people were obviously mad. Who let them run around like this, hungry and dirty?

The leader rode up to the fire and stared down at Varina. Several of his cohorts followed. Then he abruptly dismounted and approached her.

"What are they going to do, Cornelius?" she asked nervously.

"Nothing, cian. You, whoever you are . . ." Cornelius stepped forward and never got to finish his sentence. With one swift, stiff arm movement, the stranger hit him, and Cornelius dropped unconscious. Behind her, Varina heard Alta and Jason cry out in alarm. The stranger reached out to grab her. Varina jumped back in anger and her red boot flashed up past the fire as she kicked him. He staggered backward and sat down hard on the pine needles. "Look out," yelled Jason. She wheeled around to deliver a second kick, this time into the solar plexus of a woman, whose breath went out of her with a great woosh and who dropped, gasping, like a beached fish.

"Let me alone!"

Alta's cry made her turn. Two people were holding Alta and Jason and were attempting to put ropes around them. She had started to their rescue when something hard and heavy struck first her head and then her back. As the wave of pain welled up, she felt herself falling onto a red world of nothingness with pine needles jabbing her right hand.

Eleven

SHE WAS AWARE of pain and jarring motion and pressure in odd places. She tried to move, but could not.
With effort, she opened her eyes. They were not focus-
ing properly; she imagined she saw the brass and red
leather of her stirrup jangling empty directly below her
head. Below the stirruplike thing was a black sandy
surface that sparkled like glass. She could hear it
snapping under horses' feet. There was a smell of
ashes, dusty ashes that kept flying up in spurts. She
turned her head and tried to raise it. Before pain ended
again in unconsciousness she knew she had been tied
belly down over a horse.

There came a roaring in her ears like the winds of
long ago when storms swept the plains of D'laak. They
have sent me back, then? came her dim thought, or am
I in the cylinder? But Cornelius's hand was on her
arm, and his voice was angry. "She'll die of cold if
she's not dead already. Close that door, you filth!"
Alta and Jason were there; she could smell them. So
she was still on earth. Still *human*. There was a familiar motion of lift-off and the roar diminished. She felt
the weight of Cornelius's cape settling over her body
and being tucked in about her before she lost
consciousness again.

"Varina, wake up. Please wake up." She could hear
Alta pleading. "I'm scared, Jason. She hasn't moved
since they hit her."

"You're scared. I've been scared ever since they
hit Cornelius. Wake up, Varina." Jason patted her on
the shoulder. They had been in some noisy thing. Now
it was quiet and warm. Why wouldn't her eyes open.
"Where's Cornelius?" she asked, and her voice
sounded strange to her.

"She said something! Varina, wake up. Please?"

"Sh-h-h, they may be listening at the door," cautioned Jason.

"Cornelius? Where is Cornelius?" It seemed to her that safety lay with him.

"Out with them. But he's okay. They're talking to him." Alta was patting her hands encouragingly, helplessly.

"Are you two all right?" she asked.

"Sure. They didn't hit us. Mostly because we didn't threaten them, I guess. Maybe we should have."

"No!" Varina's eyelids finally obeyed the impulse and opened to see her friends standing behind her, looking worried and dirt encrusted, but whole and unharmed. She reached out and touched first one, then the other, to make sure they were real.

There was no question about the room's reality. She would never imagine a place like this. It was a lounge furnished with shabby folding chairs and scuffed tables. The dirty green ceiling was water stained.

"Where is this place?"

Jason shrugged, "We don't know. West of where we camped. . . . We rode horseback until dawn, and then a strange aircar picked us up and we flew about one hour."

Varina tried to calculate. "At least one hundred miles by air—maybe twenty by horse?"

"Not that far," Alta said, "it was slow going."

"Yeah, we got to see where the flashes were," Jason remembered. "There's a burned strip about ten miles wide!" And, seeing the question in her eyes: "We decided you were right; we did cross the boundary back there! There was some kind of fight that night we saw the flashes. Cornelius thinks at least three towers aren't working—that they broke them somehow."

"They? Who? It makes no sense." Varina was confused. "Who . . ." She tried to think and in her agitation sat up abruptly. The room went around in slow sickening circles, and she grabbed Alta's hand.

"You okay?" Alta tried to peer into her eyes as if to spot the problem. Varina grinned in spite of the pain that throbbed through her back and head. "I will be," she said.

"The woman who looked at you said you had—something about an anatomy?" said Alta and explained, "See, after the bigman in the blue uniform came in to see you . . ."

Varina held up her hands. "Stop. Start with how we got here—wherever this is. What happened then?"

"We . . ."—Jason thought back—"that was this morning. We landed at the airpad here—this is sort of mountainy desert country—and we were brought to this building."

"It's a very strange house," interjected Alta, "made of wood and bricks. And there are a lot of people here like the ones you saw. Dirty."

"They brought us in here," continued Jason. "Cornelius carried you. They shoved us in and gave us water and let us use the bathroom. There's no soap or towels. And then everybody who hadn't seen us got to come in and stare and talk about us."

"They don't like us," said Alta. It seemed to bother her. She had always been approved of.

"And then a big aircar came, and this tall man came in. Everybody called him governor, but he wasn't wearing ruling colors. Just a blue uniform."

"He's handsome enough to be a governor, I guess," Alta added, "but he doesn't act like one. Nobody bowed to him or anything."

"When he came in he just looked at us three and shook his head like he didn't want to believe we were here. Then he came over and looked at you. And the funny thing is, as soon as he saw you, he said, 'Varina!' as if that really surprised him. Then he asked us if that was your name. But he already knew you. Who is he?"

Varina shook her head and wished she had not.

"Well, he sent for a medic and asked the people who brought us here a lot of questions, and he seemed angry at them. When it started to get interesting he remembered we were listening, even though we could hardly understand when he spoke with them. . . ."

"They talk funny," said Alta. "It's our language but . . . different."

"He went outside, and then he opened the door and called Cornelius 'escort' and said, 'Would you please come with me, sir. I think we should talk.' That's where Cornelius is now."

Varina nodded and tried to sort out all this information. They had crossed the boundary—and traveled west. That would put them in sector nine. About one hundred and twenty miles inside.

The door opened and Cornelius came in. He was unshaven; he looked dusty and very tired; then he saw Varina sitting up, and his face brightened.

"Cian, you have no idea how glad I am to see you awake! Are you—can you walk?"

"I am well," she assured him. "Thank you for your cape, and for your care."

Cornelius shook his head sadly. "Your guardian will not express any gratitude for the care I've given you on this trip."

"But I will," she said, and held out her hand to grasp his. "Thank you. Are you all right?"

"Well enough, I guess. I'm not hurt physically." His teeth flashed white in his sunburned face as he laughed. "I never realized how sheltered a life I led. We all . . ." A cloud seemed to pass over him, and he paused and then said, "We are prisoners, cian. Prisoners of a war we didn't even know was happening."

"War is not allowed." She spoke automatically. "What sector is involved? Who is quarreling with whom?"

"It involves all sectors, from what I can gather. Against Kelador. The governor said they were going to take over Kelador."

She stared at him. It made no sense to her. Kelador ruled this world . . . and then she remembered Jason saying three boundary towers were destroyed. The

54

Ruling House was all powerful. So she had been taught. At the first hint of serious unrest the drones could be activated from the palace. The governors had only to call for help. The governors . . .

"Who is this man who calls himself governor? What did he say to you?"

Cornelius paced twice about the room before answering carefully. "For all I know, he is the governor of this sector. He travels in a state car. He asked me a lot of questions, most of them about you, cian. And he seemed to know the answers before I told him, to know not only you, but the Ruling House and Kelador. I believe he was raised there. He has the manner, the air . . ."

"He was my companion?"

"I believe so."

"Do you remember him?"

"He is about my age, cian," he reminded her. "I was not in palace service at that age, but in school. We would not have met." He paused as if wondering if he should say more and decided it would not be indiscreet. "He asked if the t'kyna still loved tigers. He called her by her familiar name as you do."

Aron? Only Aron had ever had the nerve to call her "Sidra"—and of all the companions, only from him had she permitted this familiarity. After he left Kelador, Varina remembered that Sidra, who paid little attention to children, mentioned this child and how well he was doing at the academy. She remembered wondering then if Sidra missed him too. For Aron had been someone special. . . .

"Cian? You're staring into space. Are you ill?"

"No—no." She pushed back the memories. "With this man as their leader, they are trying to invade Kelador?"

"From the rubble we rode through, yes. Apparently the boundary is being tested and weak spots have been found."

"But how? Without the Ruling House seeing? What about the automatic controls?"

"It has been a long, long time since Kelador had to worry about its boundary. They take fear for granted. . . ." Cornelius paused to select his words. "The best of us get careless. Equipment deteriorates. . . . I don't give him much chance of success, though. And if the people we flew over were his army, I pity them. He must have every man, woman, and child over fourteen headed toward the boundary."

"On foot?"

"Lots of them," said Alta. "I never saw so many people walking."

"Or machines," said Jason, "great awkward machines."

"Mining equipment," Cornelius explained.

"His people must be very loyal to obey a mad command like that," said Varina.

"If it was a command," he said. "The man is all too sane."

Varina looked at him, but Cornelius's face was expressionless. "Why, Cornelius? Why would a governor and his people attack Kelador?"

"The governor did not say, cian."

Varina changed the subject. "We must get away from here somehow—get back across the boundary, or find a videocom and warn Sidra. . . ."

The door flew open so hard it slammed against the wall, and a hostile-looking woman stood in the opening. "You're to come with me," she ordered. Cornelius helped Varina to her feet.

"You know what?" said Jason. "Going to the academy will seem pretty tame after this."

There were two armed guards waiting outside to escort them. The woman led them down a red dirt lane between ramshackle buildings. Varina's impression was of a crude village. Even with Cornelius supporting her arm, it was all she could do to walk and move as if she were not in pain. Waves of vertigo kept blurring her vision and balance. Between blurs she would carefully commit the immediate terrain to memory to avoid stumbling. There were people standing about, and pine trees, and mountains poked up over the pines. She would look at them all when her eyes focused properly.

They crossed an unkempt lawn and a driveway and came to a gate in a high brick wall. The gate was opened for them. Within stood a large pink brick building, graceless amid its flowerbeds, fountains, and lawn. It was here they were taken.

The first floor appeared to be administrative offices, staffed by uniformed workers or soldiers. It was a cheerless place. They were hurried up a back stairs and down a corridor to a small suite of four rooms. The clothing and personal effects from their packs were piled on the beds. There was common garb in the closets. "Do not leave your rooms," the woman ordered as she left them. "Our people are not friendly to your kind."

So far as Varina was concerned, the only good thing about these quarters were the bathrooms. She was soaking in a tepid bath within a few minutes.

To soap her shoulder caused pain, as did touching both shoulder and head with the towel. A look in the mirror revealed ugly bruises. There was a lump on her head; it hurt to brush her wet hair. She had never been deliberately hurt; until that struggle yesterday she had never tried to inflict damage on another creature. Knowing that she had been involved in both made her feel diminished. That feeling intensified when, as she was dressing, the order came that she was to dine with the governor. Not an invitation. An order.

Twelve

THE GOVERNOR'S SUITE was on the other side of the building, an area markedly more luxurious than the guest quarters. Deep velvety carpets, soft lighting, and precious wood paneling all served to shut out harsh

57

reality. The guard who escorted her there pressed a hidden bell chime, bowed, and departed.

The door swung silently open upon a room that might have been in the palace. The carpet was an art treasure, the table centuries old; there were crystal and porcelain, the scents of lemon, beeswax and freshly cut flowers. It was a room of symmetry and grace such as few of earth's people ever saw or knew existed. She stood in the doorway taking it all in. This governor might be of the people, but he lived like a Delikon. The door lock clicked shut behind her.

"Varina!" The man rose from a chair by the fireplace and hurried toward her with arms outstretched as if to welcome an old friend. Recognition came as a shock. It *was* Aron—or it had been. But what had happened to him? For a moment she thought irrationally that this aged body was hiding the person she knew, that he had been deliberately restructured to look this way and now was trapped inside that skin and could never change back.

To save him the indignity of her pity, she hid behind formality. "I am of the House of Kelador, governor. It is customary to address me by my title," she said.

He stopped, and she knew she had caused pain. His smile did not quite fade, but his arms dropped to his sides. "Yes, cian." His voice was tired. "I know. Protocol. Order. Kelador does not change, does it? You do not change. Unfortunately we do. We grow up. We grow old. . . ."

Crossing to a sideboard, he pressed a service button on the wall and then poured two drinks, an amber liquid over ice and a glass of apricot juice. She noted and found touching the fact that he remembered her preference for apricot. "Please sit down," he suggested, as he brought her the juice and settled himself back in his original chair. "You don't know me, do you?" That fact seemed to sadden him. "I am Aron. Or perhaps I should say I *was* Aron . . . many years ago when I was sure of things like that."

"I know." Her reply was hardly audible.

Mercifully there was a knock on the door. Two servants entered with a serving cart. As she watched them prepare dinner, her mind saw only Aron . . . as he had been. What could have happened to him, and when did this terrible thing happen that lined his face and made his eyes so sad? In only forty years? Such a little time within her life. But not in his. Obviously not in his. So this was why she was not allowed to meet her companions ever again.

And because it grieved her she wondered for a moment if this whole fantastic adventure had been engineered by Sidra to teach the teacher a lesson, to make her glad to go home. "Their life span is to ours as their pets' lives are to them. . . ." But Sidra was never cruel. Ruthless, but not cruel.

"I'll serve. Thank you." Aron's voice and the noise of the door closing behind the servants broke into her thoughts. He was watching her, gauging her reactions by some scale she could not measure. When their eyes met he looked away, down into the amber liquid in his glass. "I'm touched," he said. "I did not think you would care enough to be so disappointed by what I had become."

For the first time in her life here, it was difficult for her to translate thought into human speech. Her grief at his changed, aged face was overwhelming. In her silence he became unsure. "You *do* remember me?"

"I remember Aron." She couldn't manage a smile, but her voice was controlled. "I remember you—and Julia . . ."

It was a game humans played—pretending to one another that they did not feel pain. She wanted to run away, anywhere, out, away under the comforting stars, lift up her head and keen with pain as any Delikon would do. Instead she took a sip of juice and made polite conversation.

"You were not the type one forgets. You set a standard of excellence. In all respects. Even the t'kyna was impressed with you. And more than a little charmed. She speaks of you still on occasion . . . of how you used to sing . . ."

A wry grin made his mouth go sideways. "Sidra? Our beautiful—what should I call her?—head priestess? I'm delighted to hear that. You see, I hope to visit her soon." He set his drink aside and got up from his chair. "Shall we eat while we talk?" he suggested. "As you probably know, Julia governs sector five. She rather disapproves of me. . . . I suppose it is embarrassing to be associated with the man who is known to be your only failure."

Varina had the feeling she'd missed something. "I do not understand."

"Myself. I'm your only failure. The only former companion of yours never given permission to reenter Kelador." He saw the expression on her face. "Surely you knew?"

"Why?" It seemed unbelievable. Of them all he was the brightest and the best.

"Why couldn't I re-enter . . . ?" He fell silent for a moment. "I don't know, Varina. I guess I was never willing to make my people pay the price. It is difficult to encapsulate all this time—to make you understand without my seeming to whimper. Because I did show promise, my assignment was here—sector nine. It's a mining region and has been for centuries. The people are all lower caste. The land . . ." He shook his head. "It makes no difference now anyhow. Suppose we change the subject. Do you like almond duck?" He passed her a plate of food.

"But I want to understand why."

He studied her face; then he shook his head again. "I don't think you can, Varina. I don't think we can ever understand each other. Your intelligence is different in a way I cannot grasp . . . your . . . concept of rationality so vast that it seems simple or naïve to me. As if your people cannot grasp the effect they have on us. There is an unbridgeable gulf. . . ."

It was like an echo of Sidra describing the tigers: "We will always be alien to one another. So it is with

60

our species and man." And then she remembered what else Sidra had said: "If they could they would kill us." Was that true for both human and tiger?

"Do you want to kill us? Is that the purpose of this war?"

His fork clinked against porcelain and he stopped in mid-thought and stared at her, then took a deep breath. "I had forgotten how direct you could be. No. I . . . we . . . don't want to kill the people of Kelador. We want to be free of your rule."

"Why?" Varina did not understand. "The history of the dominant intelligence on this planet was chaos until we enforced order and discipline." She saw Aron nod as if her words confirmed some suspicion of his.

"But you are enforcing an order and discipline not suitable for humans, Varina," he said, his tone a plea for her understanding. "It may seem entirely logical to a superior race, if that is what you are. And as I look at you, it seems obvious that it is a social order designed for people with very long lives, a people to whom change would be not only unnecessary, but a threat to the learning process. We are never told how Kelador assumed command. I am sure that that omission is deliberate. Or perhaps the old myths are true. But your people have failed to comprehend a very important thing about us—*we do not have the time to learn*. Look at you. Then look at me!"

He pointed to their reflections mirrored in the window. The room was very still. From the floral centerpiece a poppy petal fell like damp silk onto the table and gleamed blood red against the polished wood.

As if in response to the stillness, the man's voice was soft when he spoke again. "You assumed the positions of gods and, like God, you left us with free will. You caged us in with rigid laws, but you failed to capture our souls. That failure will destroy Kelador, if not this time then in time to come."

She had been listening carefully. They had not been wrong; Aron did have a good mind. But it seemed to go so far and no further. Then it took refuge in talk of souls and gods, human supernatural symbols. Perhaps he was right, as Sidra was right—but in such different ways. If Aron was correct . . . She had instructed her companions as she would a lesser Delikon. And they had appeared to absorb her teaching. But perhaps she had created something perverse. Or was it only this one?

He saw her studying him and smiled. "You do not agree with me, do you?"

"I know nothing of the world outside Kelador," she admitted. "From your perspective you may be justified in some of your conclusions. But my people are very thorough. We seldom make mistakes."

He smiled again, this time to himself, and they ate for a time in silence.

"In your analysis of our differences," Varina said after some thought, "you were very objective. Yet it seems odd to me that I am here. Is my capture deliberate on your part?"

"Did I order your capture?" The man shook his head. "No. My people found your party by accident. I apologize for their rough treatment. You frightened them so—as it did me to see you again. But I'm glad you're here, Varina. Out of danger when the real fighting begins."

"I fail to understand what you hope to gain," she said. "Kelador's boundary cannot be crossed. You will merely physically destroy your people. To waste their lives, the acquired knowledge . . ."

"When you speak of time and knowledge wasted, you speak of your own kind. Not of the rest of us. We merely serve you—serve Kelador."

"But so do I. I served you as teacher. I prepared you for the position and power you hold now. Because you belonged there—or it was thought you did—as I belong in my position." Now *she* was pleading for understanding.

"Then you are as much a victim of the Ruling House as we are. Perhaps more so." He saw from her expression her total disagreement, and he laughed, then quickly apologized. "Forgive me. I'm not laughing at you, but at myself, at this whole situation. You see, I often imagined we would meet again. I know it's not done, but fact never stopped a man from fantasy. And in my fantasy I saw how impressed you would be with me. With all I had become."

"What have you become, Aron?" She truly wanted to know.

There was no accusation in her question, but he heard accusation nonetheless, and it angered him. "Disappointed! That's what I've become. You let us grow up thinking all people are kind; believing, for example, that a love of learning and music is universal; expecting people to speak with intelligence or at least civility. You taught me to think life would be like Kelador. And then you sent me to the academy. It was as if I had been sent into exile—away from everything that mattered! I loved you. When I was sent away, I went on loving you, trying to do what would please my image of you. For years not ten minutes passed without my missing you. Where you were was peace, was home. . . . And then I grew up. And I learned it was all part of the program. That no one else cared."

"But I did care," said Varina. "I did love you."

"Yes." His voice was sad again. "I suppose you did. It was your duty. But I loved you all by myself, without duty. I know you tried to make us whole, complete. But you see, few real people are. All of us have some gap in the circle, some cog missing in our gears. We should be warned that life is full of dull stupid people, sewer contracts, roads to be maintained, minerals to be mined. We should have been told . . ."

He was making her feel guilty, but she was not sure of what, as if she were responsible for his life. She regretted his pain but resented his weakness. "That was a long time ago in your life, Aron," she gently reminded him. "Surely you have loved others, learned enough to lessen your disappointment at having to grow up? Is it possible we misjudged you so that you reject all you were taught? If that is so, your rule would be no improvement over Kelador's."

"You can't do that to me any more, teacher," he said. "I'm long past that stage of idealism, even if you are not. And I remember the lesson of the spiral caves; in time I even came to understand it. I can accept my exact worth in relation to time, my place in what you call cosmic order. But I cannot ask my people to subordinate their own short lives, their own small satisfactions for the sake of a goal that might possibly be reached in twenty or two hundred generations. Your people have analyzed us in every possible physical and psychological way. But you no more understand us than I understand the wants and needs of a tree on the lawn."

"And what do you personally hope to gain?" asked Varina. "Kelador as you remember it?"

He was quiet for a long time and then he said, "No. I am not so big a fool as that. I know my entry into Kelador may permanently destroy what I want most, its peace and beauty. So if my army wins, I lose. No, Varina, what I hope to gain is our freedom to re-create chaos, human chaos, and from it some human goals, goals achievable in our own lifetimes."

He looked over at her perfect beauty, untouched by any expression; she was simply studying him, and he grinned at her. "Since you won't understand—why not have some more duck and help me celebrate our reunion? Three weeks from now or sooner, we will dine together again, in Kelador. I'll take you back with me."

Thirteen

HER FRIENDS WERE ASLEEP on the sofas when Varina came in, as if they had tried to wait up for her and could not. She did not waken them, but got the bed blankets and covered them against the chill mountain air. It was just as well they slept. It gave her time to think, and to see what their chances were for escape.

She went from room to room and checked the windows. All were barred from the outside. The only exit door was locked, and a sentry could be heard moving about in the hall.

Turning off the lights, she opened the blinds and one window and stood there looking out. The scents of freshly worked flowerbeds and lawns drifted in, along a faint night song of insects. A black scallop of hills stood out against the dark blue sky. It was a moonless night, and mist obscured the stars. Off in the distance a few pinpoints of light twinkled. A bat twitted somewhere near the house. From a place near one of the lights a dog barked. After a lull, the bark was answered from farther away. The sounds were isolated, alone. Behind her in the dark Cornelius began to snore softly.

Varina shivered and a feeling of extreme fatigue swept over her. She had reached out to close the window when another sound caught her attention—footsteps on a gravel path. A sentry in the garden? But these steps slurred. Two forms darker than the night moved along the faint gray of the path. The footsteps halted below the windows, and she heard a man speaking so softly she could not understand the words. Straining to listen, she caught snatches.

". . . probably worn out . . . asleep immediately." That was Aron's voice. The other man asked a question, and there was a tone of bemusement in Aron's answer. "Have you ever had a memory appear intact before you? . . . crystallized? . . . old grief you thought you'd buried long ago."

The other man said something in a placating tone, and Aron agreed. ". . . as much a victim of them as we are . . . never see reality . . . no wish to harm her . . ."

The gravel scrunched as they moved on.

The gate hinges sang out, a car door slammed. A few seconds later headlights swept over a wall and flashed over black treetops as the car turned and dipped into the valley. Then a cone of light followed by an amber bar moved up a hill and disappeared over the crest.

How very odd that he should pity her. Or was that human pretense also? She could not be sure, she who had never doubted knowledge once acquired. For a time tonight she had been sure he knew who and what she was, what the Ruling House was, and the Delikon's ultimate goal. But he was guessing. Yet he made her feel great sadness for the lost child whose anger he had revealed tonight. Was it still that child who wanted vengeance for a lost ideal, a child grown to power who now threatened the order of Kelador? Was it as simple as that? And as sorry? And would Alta and Jason mature into this form? Absent-mindedly she closed the window and went into a bedroom.

Stretched out upon a bed, fully dressed and sure she would not sleep, she studied the puzzle of Aron. Was she at fault; was it her error? Or the academy's? The teacher sketched the symmetrical outline of learning on the minds of her companions; the academy completed the picture; the apprenticeships provided practical application. Was one phase out of balance, or was Aron? Her neck and shoulders ached against the pressure of the pillow and she pushed the pillow to the floor. When she shut her eyes she saw this face with Aron's eyes looking sadly out at her. She tried to open her eyes to escape, to get away. In her dream, she was running with the winds across the plains of D'laak, free again and whole, light and swift. The lightning of a distant storm cracked brief white lines in a pale green sky as she leaped across the boulders and crushed sweet-smelling sedge beneath her. The remembered scent of grass and soil caught her and wrenched her awake again to loneliness. And in that strange room in that strange building on this strange world, she was stricken with a homesickness so acute that she nearly moaned aloud in pain. She had to get free from these earthlings, from their emotional wants and needs, from this loneliness they exuded, this failure she had helped to perpetuate. Sidra was right; they had waited too long, kept her here too long, and she was beginning to change, to mature.

She was not human, in spite of association, in spite of this human form. Her mind had not been altered, could not be. She was a Delikon. And she would willingly do now what had to be done. "In an evolved society the individual is an integral part of the whole healthy organism. . . ." She could taste again the lessons assimilated in the House nursery. Sometimes, in her sleep, the memories of her House came back. One was never lonely there and had no need to be alone. The t'kyna lived and all were separate, together and one. There was great peace in it. She had to return to Kelador, to go home again, to become whole again.

Fourteen

SHE SLEPT LATE and, thanks to Cornelius, was undisturbed until midmorning, when a guard detail arrived with the order that she appear before the governor—immediately. Fifteen minutes passed before she was ready to join them, still wearing the clothes of the night before, and without benefit of breakfast.

They led her downstairs and through the staff office. Those on duty stared as people always did. This added to her irritation at being wakened again to ugly reality. She met each hostile or curious stare with a glance that judged and dismissed. The trauma of the night before had had its effect; her close identification with humans was lessening.

The conference room was large and bare, its only decoration the pastel uniforms of the twenty-one people seated at the long oval table. Faces turned toward her as she entered. All were familiar. The last time she

67

had seen them was in the sanctuary dining room. She had not imagined their hostility that night; it was quite real, and now they made no attempt to mask it.

The only nonhostile face was Aron's. His look was more quizzical, curious to learn what effect the sight of this group would have on her. Varina stood expressionless, silently studying face after face. As her eyes met theirs, they looked away, some in anger, others in guilt, and a few in disgust.

"You were all companions?" she asked, and knew the answer before Aron spoke.

"We were all companions." Aron rose from his chair at the head of the table. "You told me once that to forgive was to condone, so I will not ask you to forgive me for bringing you to this meeting, cian. My justification for inflicting this indignity upon you is my wish for you to understand that I am not alone in my belief that the rule of Kelador must end. All of us here believe that."

Before Varina could reply a woman with steel-blue hair and an icy voice spoke up. "Who cares if she understands? I don't! My only question concerning her is what to do with her."

"Kill her. That would be the wisest plan. Systematically dispose of all her kind," softly suggested the sweet-looking old man who had only two days before assured Alta that nothing was wrong.

"Don't be a fool. Suppose we lose? She's the perfect hostage."

"What more can we lose? We've been regressing for three hundred years."

"She is so beautiful. It seems a waste to . . ."

"With her kind out of the way, our sectors are truly our own. We can all live as we please."

"With the wealth of Kelador ours," said the sweet old man.

"And how would we divide that wealth?" Aron asked quietly. "Among the people? Or will it be mine if I enter with my armies? The wealth and the power? If I choose to reward my own people with it, will any of you protest? Or stop me? Have you planned beyond conquest other than for yourself? For I have."

Abrupt silence fell. Varina was forgotten. Aron smiled to himself. "That was for your benefit, cian. I have just demonstrated the level of our understanding of power. Do you understand now what I was trying to tell you last evening?" He spoke as if they were alone.

"That you are not unique? That I failed?" she said. "Yes, I understand." Her voice was low and charged with emotion. "I understand that you have learned nothing but love of power and a taste for luxury. We overestimated our ability to teach, and human ability to learn. You would destroy the order Kelador imposes and call chaos freedom. There is no freedom without discipline, no excellence without order, no life without purpose. You would eliminate the castes and call that equality. Equality does not exist in any living form, only in atoms or chairs! I understand your goal is self-rewarding destruction; our goal is the advancement of the species into a truly social animal, with the time and discipline involved stretching over generations. Can you understand that?"

Before he could answer the woman with blue hair spoke in anger. "I understand we're being lectured to by a beautiful brat. We're not children now; we don't have to listen and smile and nod. You may be in love with the past, Aron. I am not! Since she is here, why can't we dispose of her as an object lesson to them?"

"Because that would be stupid as well as cruel," he said, without looking at her, his attention still with Varina. "Sometime, cian, when this is over, I shall show you *our* world. I shall show you how little ethics mean in the face of endless near-poverty, how lovely theories have no charm to people forced to live monotonous lives. I shall show you sector nine."

Turning again to the other governors, he said, "You wished to see the teacher who wandered into our midst. You have. Her presence here is unexpected, but I personally welcome it—and her companions. When we take Kelador, we will need her. Many of our people hold the Ruling House in high regard. You may consider their veneration simple-minded, but the fact remains that they would be appalled by a wanton destruction of Kelador. It's the most beautiful concept in their lives. What better proof of our good faith could we give them than to put this lovely child in power? As a figurehead, of course, but a very necessary one. I'm convinced she would be a popular choice. As you built temples to your teachers, so I built several to Varina. The beauty of her image alone has made them very popular."

"How clever of you to be so farsighted," observed one of the men. "Almost as if you knew she would be here when the time arrived. What a lucky accident that her escort got lost."

There was an ugly undercurrent in the words like none Varina had ever heard. It made her uneasy. She had always considered humans harmless creatures, but they rather obviously were not. They could be dangerous, not only to her, but to each other. No one had ever told her that.

The woman with blue hair rose and approached to examine her at closer range. The others watched silently, expectantly. Varina watched the woman circle her as she would watch a tiger on the loose.

"You were always an idealist, Aron. And an elitist. Either may prove fatal—like your somewhat confused sense of honor. I don't always understand you, but I trust you." She looked at the faces around the table. "At least more than I trust the rest of us. As for her" —she gave a nod in Varina's direction—"for now you can keep her. If we fail, the punishment Kelador might inflict can well be imagined. If in addition to failing we kill one of her rank, there will be no question of mercy for any of us. We will all die." She paused either for thought or dramatic effect, Varina was unsure which. "But if we win, as I think we will, and if this girl is what you claim she is . . . then I want her killed. I want no more immortal queens!"

70

Fifteen

WHILE SHE WAS BEING ESCORTED back to her quarters, Varina considered escape. It would be easier if she could go alone, at least the initial getting away. On her own world, she weighed more than twice as much as she weighed here on this low gravity planet. Beneath this skin she wore now was the same musculature that enabled her to run with ease at home. With her weighted boots, she could kick both guards into unconsciousness, and, by removing those boots, outrun any earth animal, provided she knew where to run and provided they did not shoot. Under the cover of night . . . but she could not leave the others behind. They might be safe here or they might not. In any case, they were her responsibility.

"We must escape," she whispered to Cornelius and the children as soon as the door to their suite locked. Cornelius pointed to the far bedroom as a safer place to talk without being overheard.

"Agreed!" he said when he had closed the door. "But what did you learn that makes escape so much more important?"

"All the governors are here, all those who were at the caves."

A humorless smile stretched the man's mouth. "So they were there not to meditate but to conspire."

Alta and Jason looked bewilderedly from Varina's face to Cornelius's. "I don't understand what that means," admitted Alta.

"It means they're planning to overthrow the central government. Revolution," said Cornelius. "What are they planning to do with us? Did they say?"

She hesitated. Alta and Jason might be frightened by the truth. "They will keep us here for a time."

71

"And then?"

She shrugged. "They have made no final decision."

Cornelius's eyes searched hers, and she was sure he did not believe her. "Very well," he said, "we won't gain anything by staying here. If we are to get away, we should do it as soon as possible. Now let's consider how we're going to go about it."

"The first thing is get rid of these palace uniforms," said Jason. "You can see us for miles in them."

"We'll wear the stuff in the closets."

"We'll need food," said Alta. "I'll save all the fruit I can."

It was a very simple plan. After dark, when a guard came to remove the dinner dishes and left the door unlocked for a moment, Varina knocked him unconscious with one kick. The four of them picked up the small packs they had readied. Varina opened the door and called to the other sentry. "Could you come here a moment? Your friend is ill." When the man stepped across the threshold, Cornelius poleaxed him. They locked the door behind them.

The hall was empty, as were the backstairs. They followed the same route out that they had followed in, and saw no one—sentry, soldier, or servant. All the lights were off downstairs, the offices deserted. It seemed highly suspicious to Varina. By the time they reached the door to the outside she was expecting gunfire at any moment. It was too easy. Someone wanted her to try to escape.

But no gun fired. They slipped out the door and into the night, keeping to the shadows along the side of the building. They stood there listening for sentries' footsteps and heard nothing but night sounds, faint voices, and guitar music. Furtively they sneaked along beside a path that seemed to lead away from the rear of the building toward a gate and outbuildings beyond. The gate was closed. Again they hid and listened, and then softly crossed the gravel and tried the gate.

"I can't open it!" whispered Cornelius.

Somewhere close by a dog began to bark. A pole light came on in the yard beyond the wall, and a woman's irritated voice yelled something at the dog. The four of them huddled in the shrubbery and prayed that no lights would come on in the office. The dog's barking subsided to a regretful whine that said it knew what it was doing; it was not its fault humans were stupid. After a few moments, the pole light went out again.

It was so dark even Varina's eyes took time to readjust. Cornelius's hand closed about her wrist. He touched her chin and turned her head to face a tree overleaning the wall, then pointed, and she understood. "What about the dog?" she whispered, and, as if listening, the dog gave an excited yelp. Again the light came on, and they heard a man's footsteps on gravel.

"Let's get down by the gate," whispered Cornelius. "If he opens it, we'll jump him."

"Or wait till he comes in and slip out past him," Varina said. They could hear the man talking to the dog, apparently thinking it had treed a small animal. The dog, encouraged by this appreciation of its alertness, began to bark again and led the human after this strange scent. A spring creaked as a trip mechanism released and the gate opened.

Varina could see the man standing there, looking through the bars into the darkness of the garden, could almost hear him wondering if it was worth the bother of coming in. But the dog pushed past him and came dancing over to her, tail wagging, whining in its throat with pleased excitement. About six feet from her, it stopped, sniffed, and began to growl deep in its throat. It had never smelled this smell before.

"Whattayah got, boy?" the man asked and hurried in to investigate.

Cornelius knocked him out with one punch. The dog gave a yelp of surprise and danced sideways to avoid getting hit by his falling master.

"Come!" Varina grabbed Alta's hand, pushed Jason

73

before her, and hurried after Cornelius, who waited until they were safely out and then shut the gate behind them. They ran in the shadows, along the outside of the wall now, until they were out of the island of light.

"Which way? Do you remember where we landed?"

"Over to the right are the garages; there's deep gravel in the turnaround. We're sure to be heard if we try to cross," Cornelius reasoned. "The aircar pad is over that way. There are barrackslike buildings down there."

"Where are the guards' quarters?"

"I'm not sure."

"Can we take an aircar?"

"Did you ever fly one?"

"No. But it looks simple," said Varina.

"It does. But I prefer to make my first flight in daylight. Let's find a land car." Cornelius set off as if he knew where he was going, and the others followed. The sound of guitar music grew louder. From the shadows of a pine grove to the east of the main building, they saw where the cars were parked. They saw them by the lights strung on the slope beyond, where a party was in progress. Aron was giving a barbecue for his staff and guests.

"We can't risk taking one of those cars," Cornelius decided. "Fifty people would see us before we got down that hill over there. If we weren't shot, we would at least be followed and caught."

"We will go back and take an aircar. I will pilot."

"No. I cannot let you take that risk, cian. I am responsible for your life."

"Will you fly it?"

"Neither of us will. It's too dangerous."

"All this world is too dangerous!" Varina was impatient to move. "Shall we stand here whispering until we are caught again?"

"I refuse to risk your lives. Or to let you risk them." Cornelius was adamant. "Kelador is not in that great a danger. And if we die doing something foolish, what good will that do anyone?" He would not be swayed.

Against Varina's judgment, they set out on foot toward the east, where Kelador lay.

When half an hour had passed after he'd heard the dog bark, but not any subsequent noise of an aircar lifting off, Aron left his guests and wandered up to the landing pad. More than a dozen craft sat there in the dark—unguarded, fast state cars of the visiting governors. None were missing. He looked up at the house, where the lights still burned in Varina's suite. "If you are going, you'd better hurry," he whispered to the night, and turned to rejoin his guests. It did not occur to him that his captives might have left on foot.

Sixteen

IT HAD BEEN a disquieting day spent listening to the auditors' reports on the colony, and the ambassadors' opinions and suggestions related to those reports. Earth as a colony had always been a financial liability, one which did not improve with time.

With relief Sidra removed the headgear she had worn all day and handed it to a servant. She disliked the confinement of the bubble helmet, the barrier it created between herself and her kind, between herself and Kiru, chief ambassador. Besides that, her head rang from the resonance of her voice trapped within the helmet. As she walked down the corridor from the green room, she absent-mindedly ran her long fingers, comblike, through her hair, as if to free it from confinement too.

In her office, she recorded her notes of the day's events and her reactions and then sat staring out the window at the twilight, where the temple roofs were making black silhouettes against a pale green sky. She still had to remind herself that on this world such a sky denoted high cold winds. Through the open window came the sound of a child's laughter from the garden below. The sound reminded her. She reached over and pressed the intercom. "Madam?"

"If the cian Varina has not yet dined, ask her to join me for dinner in my private quarters."

"Very well, madam."

She leaned back in the chair, wondering how Varina had parted with her companions and feeling sorry for her. This evening would be another ordeal for the child.

The intercom hummed. . . . "Madam?"

There was a long pause, and Sidra felt a flick of irritation. "Yes?"

"I am told that neither the teacher nor her companions has returned. Nor has the escort Cornelius."

"That is improbable."

"I will check further. . . ."

"Call the housekeeper. Check with the transport dispatcher."

"I have checked. With both. The pilot sent to pick them up waited a full twenty-four hours. He then surveyed the area. . . ."

"Did they leave the caves?"

"On schedule."

"Send the pilot to me." Sidra was on her feet and pacing. The inactivity of the day combined with this news suddenly created great tension in her.

She would not have run away, Sidra thought—and in thinking that admitted her suspicion that Varina could have. She is not that disturbed. Besides, where would she run to? Any of them? Cornelius would not allow harm to come to her. Could they be lost? But she doubted that. Where was that pilot, and why hadn't she been told of this before? She forgot she had been in meetings for days, unavailable to her staff.

When the pilot was shown into her office ten minutes later she verbally pounced on him. But all her questions revealed was that he had spent hours searching for his missing passengers; that neither the sanctuary nor the mountain stable where the horses were to be returned had any further knowledge of the four. He suggested they had become lost in the mountains.

"Ridiculous!" Sidra said. "No one from the Ruling House gets lost. Why did you come back without them? Why?"

"I am due for transfer, t'kyna. My restructuring starts in the morning. I have been here two terms."

"And the teacher has been here nine, in immature form. You can wait another day or two. I want pilots with earth service out there—the new ones know nothing about terrestrial geography. You will all go out in the morning." She turned on the intercom. "Notify all western boundary towers in the area of the teacher's party. I want reports of anything unusual. Send a guard contingent to the sanctuary landing and have them make a thorough ground search, to the boundary, if necessary." She dismissed the pilot with, "Get some rest. You will be up before dawn." She switched on the intercom and ordered all staff back on duty.

Disturbing reports began to come in within the hour. Two towers reported freak electrical storms. Several reported having fired on trespassers from sector nine. Three towers overlooking sector nine did not respond to voice or video contact. Sidra ordered all towers to be contacted. A total of seven did not respond. Yet all showed routine operational checks at their scheduled hours. All videocom contact outside the borders of Kelador brought only a test pattern.

Something was very wrong. For the first time she allowed herself to consider that harm from an outside source might have befallen Varina. But who would dare to harm one who wore the royal colors? Or perhaps noncontact was due merely to atmospheric disturbances. A quick check with the observatories ruled that out. It was then she ordered all weather photos of the past week for Kelador and the bordering areas enlarged and scanned. By three that morning she knew some of the answers and she took them with

77

her to the green room to advise Vashlin and the visiting dignitaries from D'laak.

"All personnel storage cells in all sectors show cold. The guards are gone. None of our bases responds. There is more. You will note from the infrared pictures the path of a tunnel bored to reach the base of tower twenty-three. Apparently personnel were overwhelmed and the tower's lasers used to destroy towers twenty-two and twenty-four. The boundary has been violated."

She flashed another picture on the screen. "This valley is six miles inside Kelador in palace forests." The valley was full of people and machines. "They have entered from the ninth sector. Our current governor of that sector has aways been an . . . innovator."

"You think they are preparing for what they consider war?" Kiru's tone was amused. "Shall I call down the taxi craft now and have them incinerate the entire area?"

"No! Have you forgotten? Varina has not returned. She may be held captive by them."

Kiru considered this. "She has sacrificed enough for this planet," he agreed, "but surely, if we had no other choice, I believe she would understand. If I did not think her so advanced, I would not have given her the Ring."

"She might, but *I* would not understand her need to die." Sidra was adamant. "I rule this world."

"Beloved t'kyna," Bader sang, "the question must now be asked: Should we continue to rule this world? So far from D'laak, so costly, and so cruel? Much have we spent here, in time and physical endurance, in wealth as well, all in the hope that humans could more quickly evolve. Could this have happened—could it happen ever—then the expense would be justified. But humankind as a species shows no evidence of maturing into a complex social being. In this primitive state, they will never grasp cosmic order. They do not want to understand. They remain the parasites who will destroy their host, with no more than a primitive grasp of order. We achieved only our initial goal. But that is enough. Humans will never again visit the stars!"

The t'kyna and the others considered this in silence.

"Then we would abandon earth after all this time?" she asked. "Is this the thought of the High House also?"

"Even before our last three audits, it had been considered," Kiru admitted. "If we left them in new chaos, it would be no different a situation than that in which we found them."

"We would all return with you to D'laak? Now?"

"Does the idea distress you?"

Sidra's great eyes fastened on his. "Distress me? No. If I had permitted myself to dream of the end to this exile, I would have dreamed of little else. Could I have allowed myself to wish, I would have wished for little else. But unless you are sincere in this suggestion, do not torture me with its promise."

"We are sincere, t'kyna," Kiru assured her.

"Then we have much to do." Sidra arose, her mind made up. "First we must find the child Varina. Arrangements must be made for restructuring all my colonial staff. . . ."

"There is the question of the remaining soldier drones," Bader reminded them.

"They were restructured specifically for earth," an auditor said. "At great expense. Their minds are useless for anything else. They were designed for close-range surface combat with armed indigenous life forms. They would be dangerous to transport. And we have no use for them at home."

"Then we will let the earthlings earn their admission to Kelador. We will loose the drones on them. That will hold them at bay until we depart," Kiru decided. "And if the humans have killed Delikon in this latest madness of theirs, the drones will serve to balance the account."

Seventeen

IT WAS SLOW GOING in the dark, especially since they
were totally ignorant of the lay of the land. Away from
the buildings, the wooded ground fell in a steep slope,
then tilted up again. Rain-washed gulleys, invisible in
the night, tripped them; barbed-wire fences caught and
held them, tree branches clawed at their clothing.
Twice deer crashed away through the thickets, the
noise of their flight unidentifiable and terrifying.
Where scrub pine gave way to meadow, ghostly white
forms loomed up out of the grass and snorted at the
scent of strangers. They had disturbed a sleeping herd
of cattle.

When the lights of the governor's house had long
since disappeared behind the hills, they stopped to
rest. There was no moon, and a thin wind had risen.
Alta and Jason were tired and cold. If Cornelius was
tired, he didn't say so. Varina was not; she wanted
only to get home.

She sat and listened to the labored breathing of the
other three and wondered how they were ever going to
make it. And she found herself thinking she might
have done them a favor by leaving them behind. They
had no supplies; only fruit to eat, inadequate clothing,
no transportation, and a long way to go. As if reading
her mind, Cornelius broke silence to whisper, "We're
going to have to fall in with somebody, if we can.
Otherwise we're really in trouble."

In the bushes an insect rasped, "Tssk!" and a cohort
answered, "Tsk-tsk." Crickets creaked in cheerful dis-
regard of human problems.

Varina shook her head. "That seems unsafe. If we
could find a car, horses, anything . . ."

"Can you ride cows?" suggested Jason, and they ignored him.

"I think we should stay here till it gets light and we can see where we are," said Cornelius. "I'm not sure what direction we're going and we can't walk far in the dark."

"That's a good idea," agreed Alta. "This grass feels like a bed to me. All we need are blankets."

"The scratches on my legs burn," said Jason, "and I'm hungry."

Varina suppressed a sigh of discouragement. Tomorrow was the sixth day. Tomorrow she should go into restructuring. Tomorrow . . .

A wren with a liquid song woke her. Gray fog filled the hollow below them and made more gray the early morning light. Her shoulder and neck ached. Sleeping in the open had made the bruise sore. Stiffly she got up and walked a discreet distance into the trees. She found a small spring welling out of the ground and washed herself as best she could. The stones of the spring were furry with rusty algal growth and the water tasted metallic. As she came back downhill she looked out across the hills. To the northwest were roofs, perhaps three miles away. If they could get there before anyone was up, perhaps they could steal some food.

The figure of a man moved among the trees below. She froze for a minute before seeing it was Cornelius. It was strange how different he looked out of uniform, older, somehow more vulnerable. On impulse she waved to him and pointed to the roofs. When he had seen them he gave her a mock salute.

Alta and Jason woke hungry and in a foul mood. Their legs were brier-scratched through their pants, and they spent a good five minutes bemoaning this desecration of their skin before it occurred to Alta to ask, "How are you, Varina. Did you get badly torn up?" and she pushed up Varina's pants leg to look. Varina's legs were flawless. "How did you do that?" Alta wanted to know.

"I never walk into brier vines," said Varina, and changed the subject. "Come on. We are going to find some food."

When they could they kept to the valleys as they walked, always close to pines in case an aircar came over. The sun was not up yet when the buildings Varina had seen came into view from the top of the hill. They were the white brick with green roofs that denoted all state property of Kelador, and when they saw that, all four felt relieved. There would be help for them there, and surely a videocom to let the palace know where to pick them up. They could see the antenna rotating on the roof of the communications building.

"Don't get careless now," cautioned Cornelius. "The governor may expect us to turn up here and be waiting for us."

"The fence is broken." Varina pointed. "All along the front. It looks like it was ripped out by a giant." Her eyes could see what theirs could not. "I think the base is deserted."

So it proved to be. The rear portion of the fence still stood, but it was not electrified. They circled around carefully until they were sure it was not a trap and then walked across the trampled meshing and onto the grounds of the base itself. The buildings stood empty, row on silent row, the grass around them long and unkempt. Disturbed rabbits bounced away to safety.

"What is this place?" asked Cornelius. "Warehouses?"

Varina thought she knew what those buildings were, but she said nothing. She was forming a plan, and she was not sure they would understand. "I will find a videocom," she said and led the way toward the antennaed building.

Its double doors were broken and hanging open. The lobby and main hall were stripped of all furniture. The offices on either side of the hall had been ransacked. What furniture still remained had been smashed. There were no videocoms; their naked wire protruded from the baseboards, and their screens were shattered glass in the walls.

The four of them trailed through the desolation room by room. "Let's see if there's anything left of the kitchen," suggested Jason, and he and Alta went off in the direction of a sign that said, "Officers' Dining Room."

Varina and Cornelius went up the debris-clogged stairs to the communications center. The destruction there was worse than below, and there was a sweetish stench in the air. Data capsules littered the floor like spilled vitamins; those stepped on left oily spots; their containers were scattered and smashed. The computer, too heavy to move or smash, had been laser-fused into a blackened lump along one whole wall. Piled in the corner in a disgusting jumble were six partially burned bodies in Keladorian uniforms.

Cornelius took one look at them and hurried outside, his hand over his mouth. Varina took time to note that they were Delikon and had been dead for a long time. The bodies had been stripped of all jewelry, all identification. Soon terrestrial bacteria would return the Delikon to their true form and then dissolve that sheath too. Only bone would remain. Unburied, far away from home. She wished for fire to purify this ugliness but of course there could be no fire. Smoke would betray them. And so she did the only thing she could: said a prayer of thanks to them for their service and sacrifice in the name of the Ruling House and of them all.

"Cian, come out of there. That's not good for you," Cornelius begged from the doorway.

"Why does the antenna still rotate?" she said, ignoring his revulsion.

"What? Oh—a sealed unit on the roof, I guess. But there's nothing left here; all the circuitry is ruined."

"Hey!" Alta called up to them. "We found some canned food. But there's nothing to open it with." She started up the steps and Varina ran down to meet her, grabbed her hand, and said, "Come on! There must

83

be something here we can punch through the lids with," as if breakfast were foremost in her thoughts.

"Did you find anything up there?" asked Alta. "Did you call the palace?"

"No. Upstairs is all smashed too."

"Maybe in one of the other buildings?"

"Maybe," Varina agreed.

After some pounding by Cornelius the cans yielded a thick, puddinglike substance that was familiarly known as "guards' gruel." Why the guards liked it was a mystery to Alta and Jason. "Now I know why they didn't bother to smash this too," Jason said, making a face as he tasted it.

"Eat it," said Varina. "It is nourishing."

With spoons salvaged from the littered floor they fed themselves, slowly and with no enjoyment despite their hunger. When they had finished they searched the kitchen storage closets for portable food. Amid the debris only two big tins of protein biscuit remained edible. They split the contents among their packs.

The sun was up when they came outside. The fog was gone. Long morning shadows stretched away from the buildings. They stood in the doorway and listened for aircraft or other human sounds and heard none. "But there could be at any minute," Cornelius reminded them. "We can't be far from Aron's place. Once they start to search they could be here in five minutes. So stay close to cover."

There were few trees on the base proper. Only buildings, most with windows broken, doors hanging open. Any supplies or equipment they might have contained were gone. It gradually dawned on the four that they would find no car, no aircraft, nothing here that would help them. But ten buildings remained closed.

They were of different design from the others, set low to the ground and windowless. Their roofs looked like black glass and an unusual assortment of vents bristled from them. Ramps led down to their doors. The doors looked like those to vaults, with wheels that must be turned to gain admittance. But the wheels spun free under Cornelius's touch as though all inner gears had been stripped.

Varina watched him try two doors with no success. On the third building, she stopped and looked the entrance over carefully. These doors were designed to keep what was inside safe from tampering. Around each door was what appeared to be a decorative strip of tile patterned in green on white and set here and there with jewel-like blobs of glass.

Jason saw her looking at them. "It's like the design on the door to the caves," he observed, "only different." As he said that the pattern of the lock became clear to her and she smiled at him in thanks. She had begun to think so much like a human that her mind had failed to see what should have been obvious. She reached up and pressed each glow-spot the required number of times. The door began to click, and small motors whined within. The outer wheel turned slowly, and the door opened.

As soon as she smelled the odor that came out that door Varina knew what was in those buildings—what she had suspected. Quickly, in case they were not all dead, she spit on her hand and rubbed it on her forehead, then dabbed Alta's and Jason's forehead, then Cornelius's as well. "Do not ask why. Trust me," she said.

"What's in there?" Alta pointed down the dimly lighted, tube-like hall that led from the door. "I am not sure," said Varina, "but I think you'd better stay outside while I look."

"I'll go look," Cornelius said, but she stepped ahead of him. "Please!" It was an order, a tone she seldom used and never to him. "You will not like what you see. You will not recognize or understand it."

"But *you* will?" the man asked.

She nodded. "And I will be safe."

Eighteen

FEAR SWEPT OVER HER in sickening waves as she slid past Cornelius and stepped into the yellow gloom. Long ingestion of terrestrial food, the breathing of terrestrial air might have altered her chemistry so much that they would not recognize her as High House. But she would have to take that chance. Before Cornelius could stop her, she closed the door behind her.

The master control board for all chambers should be in this anteroom. But it was so dark with the door closed. She searched for the light switch and when she found it, nothing happened. One by one she pushed the buttons on the control panel. Nothing lit up. Stepping back, she looked down the hall to see how it was lighted; it was the glow of sunlight through the strange roof. Then she noticed the dials on the monitoring equipment. All had fallen to zero.

"The building is dead." She spoke aloud in shock. "They are all dead. They must be . . ." Her glance fell on the inventory plaques on the wall, where the High House of D'laak promised that encapsulated in these cells one hundred and eighty-one defender drones waited in a dormant state to come to the aid of the Ruling House of Kelador should insurrection rise in sector nine. Pathetically detailed instructions followed—on the order in which chambers were to be activated for maximum effectiveness, on which songs were to be sung.

She could hear the dim thuds of Cornelius hammering on the outside door. There was no sense worrying him. She might as well go out. A short walk down the hall convinced her of the wisdom of that. All the panels had sealed in place. It was the hallway of a crypt.

When she opened the heavy door and emerged,

Cornelius greeted her with, "Don't you ever do that again! What if something had happened to you? I'm responsible for you. I care about you!"

"I am sorry," she said, and she truly was. His distress was as real as his anger.

"Hey," called Jason from several buildings down. "This door is open and you ought to see what's in here!" By his tone she knew that building was dead, too. They must all be dead, every building.

Cornelius grabbed her arm and kept her from running. "What is it? You're going to have to tell me."

She turned and looked up at him, her eyes brilliant in the morning light, and as she turned she straightened and it seemed to the man that she grew—was it older? —as he watched. His hand loosened its grasp on her arm and he shivered without knowing why.

"Come and look!" pleaded Alta from the building where she and Jason had found the door open.

"Yes," said Varina. "You must see them, Cornelius. You will not understand until you do. For they were part of human myth; none have walked this world since the final war. And perhaps none shall ever again. For they are as old as Kelador. You were right, loyal escort. Kelador has grown very careless."

She took his hand and walked with him to where Alta and Jason waited, and it was no longer clear which was the protector, man or child.

"I don't know what they kept in here but I think it was animals of some kind," Jason said by way of greeting. "It's hard to tell; everything's smashed up." He and Alta led the way inside, and the other two followed.

There was an odor of sweet dryness, as if honeyed herbs had been stored here in great quantity. The control panels in the ante-room had been fused. Through the open doorway, where row upon row of octagonal cylinders had rested behind sliding panels, now only a tangle of ruin remained from the implosion that had devastated the interior. The panels were gone; not a cylinder remained intact. Parts of the roof were blown away and blue sky shone above.

"Look at this, Varina." Jason struggled to pick up what appeared to be part of a huge breastplate of opaque golden armor. "And this." He held up a helmetlike piece. "There's stuff like that all over."

"It is not stuff," Varina said quietly. "There were one hundred and eighty-one drones stored here. Living creatures. Intelligent creatures. This is what remains of them. Their outer sheaths and skeletons."

Cornelius picked up a skull casing, held it at arm's length for a moment, then hastily put it down. "What in the world were they?" he whispered. "What in heaven's name . . ."

"Do they frighten you?"

He met her eyes and nodded.

"They were bred for that. These were the sleeping armies that waited in storage bases around the world to keep humans from going to war." She pointed to the remains. "If this frightens you, the sight of a living drone would terrify you—as it should. They are deadly if they fail to recognize you as friend. At least one finger contains a laser; each claw is a knife. They can run. . . ."

"That's why you put spit on us. . . ." Alta almost whispered the understanding to herself. "So they'd know we were with you. But why would they know you?" And because of this remark Varina wondered if Alta's mind was making a connection between the ambassadors who had visited Kelador and these fragments. She also knew the time might come when Alta would ask, "What are you?" But Cornelius would never ask.

"They are coded to recognize members of the Ruling House by scent. Like great dogs," she said.

"What can they do that's so frightening?" said Jason. "I mean, if they're so great, how come they're all dead?"

"I am not sure," Varina admitted. "I have never seen one like this awake. They were never needed before. I do not know how the governor managed to shut off the power to these storage chambers. . . ."

"If that first building full of them had been alive, cian—what were you going to do?"

"Activate them and send them to stop Aron."

"How? What would keep them from killing us?"

"I would," she said firmly.

"But these things are monsters!"

Then so am I, Varina thought, as your kind once looked to me. Aloud she said, "No, Cornelius. They are just what they were meant to be—a means of defense. People killed those guards. Was that less than monstrous?"

"What guards?" Jason looked from her face to Cornelius.

"It's no matter now." Cornelius stood up. "I think we should . . . Listen!" The riffle of an aircar engine pulsed through the hole in the roof. "Get back in the control room. And don't look out the door!"

A shadow raced across the roof as the craft circled low overhead, and then they heard it whine down and land.

"Where?" Alta whispered.

"By the main building, I think," Jason replied.

"Sh-h-h-h."

The silence was heavy as the motor shut off. Even the few insects in the grass fell still. There was a faint tinkle of breaking glass as a derelict door slammed, followed by a few unintelligible shouts. Then, so close they held their breaths in fear, a man's voice said, "How about in there?"

"Nah! Whattaya think, kids are gonna hide in that stink? Would you?"

"Guess not. The old man's wrong. She ain't here. None of 'em are."

"Not now anyhow. We're wasting our time."

"They didn't get away without help. One of the old man's high-caste friends had something to do with it. I'm betting they're in sector six by now. . . ."

The voices receded in the distance, and the hunted

89

allowed themselves to breathe again. "Let's hope he can convince the others of that," Cornelius muttered.

Apparently he could not. For more than an hour they waited until the searchers were satisfied and the aircar lifted, circled the base repeatedly, and finally left the area. Then, for fear the takeoff had been a trick to lure them from hiding, Cornelius made them wait two hours more.

Nineteen

"HOW COME nobody lives here?" Jason wondered.

Three hours had passed since they left the base, and in all that walking they had seen no houses or even a road—just endless poor mountains of scrub pine and brush, sparse grass and half-wild beef cattle.

"It's probably part of the governor's land," guessed Cornelius. He had been very quiet since hearing about the drones. "I think we were at his summer home. It's cooler up here."

"This is cool?" Alta wiped the sweat from her forehead with the back of her arm and adjusted her pack.

"Listen!" said Varina.

"I hear them."

"No, not the cicadas, motors."

"Wait here." Cornelius walked on ahead toward a bluff, where he stood for some minutes gazing down, then waved for them to join him.

"There's a road down there," he reported, "a major highway from the looks of it."

They could see a short stretch of roadway where it snaked around a curve between the hills. Passing along it, heading east, were supply-trailer trains, four to six units long, pulled by squat tractors. All units were painted in splotches of grays and browns.

As they watched, the tractors began to slow and

pull onto the far shoulders of the road, where deep ruts had been cut into the gravel. The drivers and a few passengers jumped down from the cabs and trailers as if glad of the chance to rest in the shade.

In the quiet, heavy motors could be heard in the distance, creeping up through the hills. The four waited silently for the vehicle to come into view, and, when it appeared, they didn't know what they were seeing.

It was a massive piece of machinery mounted on uncountable wheels. Its body overhung the road by a good fifteen feet on both sides. The front end looked like a giant oblong mouth full of metallic teeth mounted on endless chains. It groaned and lurched like a living thing as it rolled along. Behind it came another identical machine and following were two wide conveyor units. No drivers could be seen; it was as if the machines moved of their own volition like great browsing beasts. As they passed from view, the pitch of engines changed one by one as the vehicles picked up speed on a downgrade.

"What was that?" Jason asked.

"Mining equipment," Cornelius guessed. "They may be using it to tunnel under the towers, or the boundary. If the tunnels are long enough they would avoid detection by air. Or they may be making roads through the mountains for the army to follow."

Varina was paying no attention. "How are we going to get to the boundary?"

"Well—" He spoke reluctantly as if unsure she would approve of what he planned. "I thought we might get a ride from one of these tractor drivers. I could say you three are my children and we're trying to find your mother. That she went off with the others . . ."

"What about my eyes?"

"You'll be wearing my sunglasses." He dug them out from his pack.

"And the way we talk?" said Jason.

"You won't talk—you're very tired. And if you

have to, slur your speech, swallow it. I can mimic them well. But then, I was not born in Kelador."

"Suppose they were told to watch for us?" said Varina.

"Ah . . . then we do have a problem. But it's either take the chance or walk."

Varina knew she would rather run—much rather. But the rest of them could not. And she doubted they could walk all the way home. Better to be recaptured than die, was her decision. Besides, even if they were recaptured, Sidra would soon set them free. Varina still had great faith in the ability of Kelador to defend itself.

It was much easier than any of them expected it to be. When they had worked their way down to the road and came walking out of the brush, one of the drivers called to them to hurry and get on if they were going on her load; she was leaving. Cornelius waved his thanks and helped the children up onto a big flatbed trailer, where they found room between an aircar engine and crates of canned food. The tractor whined to life, and they lurched out over the ruts and onto the road.

"Just follow my lead," Cornelius muttered. "If anyone talks to us, let me answer. Or just smile. Stay out of sight all you can."

From behind the shield of the sunglasses, Varina studied the few passengers she could see. They seemed to be strangers to one another; none of them were talking. Like the people at Aron's, these were shorter and more worn looking than the humans she was accustomed to seeing. They showed no more interest in the scenery than they did in their fellow humans, but seemed simply to be enduring a journey. She wondered where they were going and why. A young man she was watching, visible between the crates, stared back at her, and Varina casually turned away, then after a moment moved closer to Alta to get out of his line of sight.

They rode sitting with their backs against the crates,

hemmed in by the motor, their only real view to the right. The road twisted through the hills for an hour or more and then down into a treeless valley where cabbage fields stretched far to the south. Robot tractors were at work, their weeder arms spanning eighteen rows. Wheeled irrigation units rolled along in a cloud of rainbows and mist. Here and there a solitary human walked and tended the machines.

The fertile strip ended in badlands, where erosion had carved deep ravines and twisting gulleys; where sand and stony clays engulfed bedrock broken in chunks and flung casually over the landscape. For the first time Varina saw the final results of the mining humans practiced wherever the coal and oil shale remained. It had created desolation.

Here the factories and workers' towns began, each with its primitive solar water and power plants, the stink of methane, mountains of ancient tailing dumps, and hills of shale dust fused to keep it from blowing in the wind. It was ugly country; it produced ugly people. It seemed to Varina that no governor could ever hope to make this land whole again. How could Aron re-enter Kelador from this? She had always thought the world was like Kelador. Now she wondered how much of it was not. And did the Ruling House know this?

As they passed through the towns, from the dreary rows of balconied apartments people watched the convoy. Some clasped their fists above their heads in a symbol of martial salute. Their pastel coveralls and the faded colors of their apartment houses glowed against the drabness of the landscape around them.

The convoy paused for a few minutes at a square in one of the towns. A few passengers got off, and more got on. From the balconies sullen people stared down at them. The smell of garlic and hot cooking oil was heavy in the air. Varina shifted nervously, made uneasy by the alien scent of poverty. Cornelius put his hand on her arm. "We'll be going again soon," he whispered.

On the other side of the flatbed a chubby woman in blue coveralls flung a roll of belongings onto the trailer floor, hoisted herself up after it, then reached down and hauled up a small child by its arms. She looked over at her four fellow passengers and smiled, self-consciously revealing bad teeth. The child pushed itself against her in shyness. Cornelius nodded at her. The tractor lurched into gear and the woman braced herself to keep from falling sideways. Cornelius muttered, "Damn!" The woman smiled nervously at him and settled herself with her gear behind her back as a pillow as they had done. The four of them feigned great interest in the passing buildings. They were afraid that she was going to want to talk.

But she did not, not for twenty minutes or more as the towns were slowly left behind and the mountains ahead grew high enough to be seen over the top of the motor in front of them. Scrub alders and cedars reappeared alongside the road and the road itself became rough and unpaved. The trailers began to bounce with bruising force, and, one by one, the passengers stood up and rode holding fast to whatever seemed secure. The chubby woman was having problems trying to hold the child and keep herself and her belongings from bouncing.

At one really bad jolt, Varina automatically reached over and grabbed the woman's arm to keep her from falling. When the road smoothed out a little and the woman had had time to think about it, she smiled at Varina and said in the vernacular, "You are as strong so you are pretty." Varina smiled slightly. Encouraged and probably lonesome, the woman repeated her remark to Cornelius and asked, "They yours?" meaning the children. When he nodded she said, "Nice. Healthy. You're lucky. Usually children that pretty are taken away."

Cornelius nodded again.

"Especially her." The woman pointed to Varina. "With those glasses on, she looks like the statue in my temple. Big eyes. Like Those-Who-Live-Forever." She obviously meant it as a compliment, but Varina saw Cornelius's face pale. "Pain," he said to the woman, pointing to Varina's glasses. "Too much sun."

"Poor thing! When we get to the camp you should take her to the hospital tent."

"Is the camp far?"

The woman shrugged. "Maybe we'll get there by dark. I'm going to cook for them. What will you do?"

It was Cornelius's turn to shrug. "What we can."

The trailers had slowed to a crawl. Ahead of them, throwing dust, were some of the big machines they had let go by earlier. When it was possible to do so, the drivers pulled off onto a sandy stretch to let the slow-moving equipment gain more distance.

Most of the passengers jumped down and headed into the brush to relieve their bladders.

"Let's go," Cornelius whispered. "Take your packs."

"Leave those. I'll keep an eye on them," the woman said as she saw them pick up the gear and Alta and Jason jumped down.

"No trouble," Cornelius smiled. His camping cup fell from his pack and Varina knelt quickly to pick it up. As she bent over her sunglasses slipped off and she picked those up too. But not fast enough. For as she raised her head the woman saw those eyes and gave a choked cry. "The statue! She's the statue!" and she fell upon her knees in an attitude of supplication. Varina stood and stared at her, dismayed not only by the attention she was attracting but by the idea of being an object of worship.

"Come." Cornelius jumped with her off the truck-bed.

"I am sorry," Varina said as they ran. "The glasses are too big. . . ."

"It can't be helped," said Cornelius. "Alta, Jason, this way. Into that gulley."

Behind them they heard a woman's scream and then shouting. Varina spurted and heard, "Cian!" and slowed. The gulley deepened into a trench overhung with alders, then angled left, and ahead of them

95

yawned the round black mouth of a storm drain. "In there," ordered Cornelius.

"No!" Varina could see no exit. "What if they trap us in there?"

"It's dark inside. They won't see us."

Alta and Jason passed her and disappeared into the black "O" and then, before she could resist, Cornelius picked her up. "If you kick me, cian, you'll break my leg," he said. It was not a plea, just a simple remark.

After the sunshine outside, the darkness of the hiding place was almost instant. It smelled of clay and bats.

Twenty

IN KELADOR fear had spread like fog across the land. And no one could say why this was. There had been few autumns more beautiful. The weather was perfect. But there were reports of strange things moving in the night. Meteors were seen repeatedly, even in daylight, arcing to the north. Herds of cattle stampeded for no apparent reason . . . until bloody piles of hides and bones were found surrounded by large, clawed footprints of nothing human. Yet no one admitted seeing such creatures.

Within the Ruling House, the staff had returned from holiday to find half their usual number missing. No explanation was given for that. Nor was it explained why the south wing of the palace plus all temples and their grounds were closed off to them . . . or who rode in the strange big cars that emerged from the temple ramp each dawn and drove off, hiding what they carried beneath shiny domes . . . or why the monitor craft took off each day like wasps swarming to the west.

Each nightfall, when the pilots had returned with

no report of Varina and more pictures of the boundary's violation, Sidra despaired. In the twilight gloom of the ambassadors' chamber, she met with Kiru on his last evening on earth. They spoke of home and the past, and of times to come. And then they returned to now. Could she have planned it, she would have preferred the end of her rule to be, if not glorious, at least a time of order—certainly not of fear.

"You should tell the people what they must expect," Kiru said.

"What is the point of explaining now?" replied Sidra. "It would only produce terror and chaos. Better to leave them in mystery. Humans respond well to mystery. They make religions of it."

"Then you must allow us to devastate the boundary area," Kiru insisted. "If we do not, the people of Kelador will have no time to prepare a defense against the invaders."

"And if Varina is among the hostiles?"

"The High House would mourn long after this world is forgotten," said Kiru, "but we must consider these people."

"Hers is the only life out there that matters to me," Sidra said and refused to give the order.

"So be it," said Kiru, but obviously did not approve. "All the drones have been released. All your staff is in restructuring, except yourself. The technicians await you. . . ."

"And Varina?"

"Like Varina, I represent the High House of D'laak. You are her guardian. I now absolve you of that responsibility. In three terrestrial days you will enter restructuring, with or without her. My ship leaves tomorrow; yours, seven days from tomorrow. All our technicians will be on that last ship. It is improbable that another ship will come to Kelador—or near this star for many earth years to come.

"I have given orders that you are to be aboard that ship. In alien or natural form. I gave this order out of esteem for you."

"You still hold me in esteem when you disapprove of my actions?"

"Always."

Sidra's sigh hissed within the bubble helmet, and she shook her head in vexation at the sound. "You must understand, house friend, I do not leave these people undefended out of anger, but with the thought that once we leave, Kelador will inevitably fall to the invaders. There is no hope that those who live here can stop that from happening. The more they resist the more of them will die."

"But what if the invaders kill them anyhow?"

"Then there is no point in adding more fear to the inevitable, is there?"

At dawn, Sidra saw the ambassadors for the last time. They met in the great hall of the Delikon temple; there they sang their prayers of flight and farewell. Around them in the hall the occupied cylindrical pillars glowed and shimmered; above, the spiral turned, white against the infinite blue. When the song had ended Kiru walked with her to the enclosed ramp where the great cars waited. This time it was he who wore the bubble helmet and she who breathed freely.

"You must let the pilots be restructured, t'kyna," he reminded her. "This must be their last day of searching. And, like them, you must stop looking, too."

"She will come back."

"Forgive me, but she is very human now. If she still lives." His strange eyes glowed down at her. "It is you I worry about, the guardian."

The car doors slid open to admit him and Bader, who followed behind.

"You will see us both again," she assured him, "looking as we were meant to look, free of all this." She pinched the soft skin of her face, pulled at the hair. "Like all good colonial servants, we shall bring home mementos of our sojourn in the primitive worlds, and possibly long at times for what we thought we endured here."

"And we shall comfort you," he said.

In their estranged forms no real farewell gesture was possible. Their hands clasped, and she saw him enter the car. By the time the ramp doors opened and the cars pulled out, she was crossing the topiary gardens on her way to her office. There was much still to be done.

Those who had released the drones and moved with them to the boundary would return today. Once the drones had scented the enemy there was no longer any need for control. The monitor craft would have to be disposed of; she had no intention of letting them remain behind to add to some human conqueror's power. Varina's few belongings would have to be packed. The two companions, Jason and Alta . . . she paused in her thoughts for a moment. What to do with them? Would these humans allow the academies to remain? The idea of their destruction was disturbing. If that happened, then all the time was wasted, all the knowledge would be lost. And the caves . . . they must be sealed, the keeper recalled, the sanctuary destroyed.

It was very still within the palace; her boot heels clicked on marble floors and echoed down long corridors. The guards on duty saluted her as she passed, shorter guards, all humans. . . . It seemed very cold this morning.

Twenty-one

THEY STAYED HIDDEN in the culvert until night, resting and dozing. When they crept out the tractor trains were gone. The road was as empty and bare as the land around them. They crossed the road and set off walking through the scrub, and soon night hid them from view. The first five miles were easy. The ground was firm, and star-light was more than adequate to see by. The mountains loomed ahead like a promise of safety urging them on. Leaving the valley, they began to climb steadily upward across a barren mesa. By midnight they were high enough to see that to the southwest were scattered clumps of lights that were either a town or a great encampment.

"That's where all that machinery was headed," Cornelius decided. "The camp where that woman was going to be a cook."

Near dawn found Varina picking her way across a talus slope. Reaching solid rock again, she sat down on the ground to rest and watched the other three approach. They were slipping and sliding, creating small avalanches of stones that went rattling off down the mountainside. She felt a surge of pity for Alta and Jason. She was tired, and she knew they had to be near exhaustion. Cornelius too was beginning to lag.

Suddenly the sky lit up as if giant fireworks had gone off. A low thundering rumble followed, and then a wind came shrieking down out of nowhere. There was a hail-like patter, and it wasn't until she was rapped on the arm by one that Varina yelled, "Stones!"

There was no place to take shelter. They fell on the ground face down, holding their packs over their heads as protection. The dust-filled wind rushed over them, tugging at the packs and flapping their clothes. Near Varina something hit the ground with a flappy thud. She risked looking over; it was a bare human leg. Shock kept her silent. At first the only thing she allowed herself to think was that Alta and Jason must not see it or, if they saw it, recognize it.

The hail stopped with the wind, and when she raised her head again, darkness had returned. She closed her eyes to refocus the lenses. She could hear distant human sounds now, shouting and some screams, and the high-frequency whine of laboring motors. From a peak hidden by the mountain ahead of them, long beams of yellow light shot down in rhythmic pulses. It was answered by repeated explosive thuds and arcs of light.

"What's happening?" Alta and Jason wanted to know as they got up and brushed themselves off.

"I think sector nine's people are trying to take a tower, and the tower is fighting back," said Cornelius. "They must have hit an ammunition supply."

"Let's go watch!" Jason said eagerly. "I never saw a battle before."

"No!" Varina was horrified. "Come on. Get up under the cliff where we have some protection. . . ." She detoured them around the obscene debris the wind had flung down. Cornelius caught up with her and half whispered, "We've got to go toward the battle to get around the cliff. Either that or walk twenty miles back north and try to get up to the boundary there."

The thought of losing that much more time made Varina desperate. She had to be in Kelador by tomorrow. "We will be safe in the darkness," she said. "No one is expecting to see us."

"Lasers have no expectations, cian," he reminded her.

"They will be aimed at the attackers," she insisted.

In the hour it took to walk around the cliff the sounds of battle grew louder. The eastern sky became blue with dawn. Where the next mountain groined to meet the mesa a small cedar grove stood. The air smelled not of pine but of smoke and dust. The trees ended in a rock outcropping.

"Look." There was joy in Jason's voice. They could see the cliff to the east, where the red beacon light of a boundary tower flashed.

"They didn't get it yet!" said Cornelius thankfully, and they headed east toward that red glow.

They could hear aircars now coming in from the west, but the craft were invisible, flying with all lights out. A searching shaft of white light shot out from the tower. They saw it strike the belly of a craft.

Instantly an amber ray pulsed. There was a starburst as the craft disintegrated. The white beam moved on, hunting. From the next valley came a barrage of explosions, and the tower base lighted up for an instant. The pulsing amber beam hovered and pierced the valley. An aircar directly above the tower dropped something which exploded. The tower's amber beam made fireworks of the attacker. The red light continued to flash. The sky behind it reflected pink from the rising sun.

"There goes Aron's air force," commented Cornelius. But he was wrong.

From the edge of the mesa the entire scene lay spread out before them. The boundary tower, flanked by a connecting wall, stood between two mountains at the eastern end of the canyon. Formed by an ancient river, the canyon had once provided a natural pass into the mountains. Directly below the place where Varina stood, the canyon was perhaps a mile across, with gently sloping sides.

Moving east toward the tower, on the canyon floor, creating their roadway as they moved, was an army of machines. A spearhead of huge bulldozers led the way, with enormous metal shields mounted on their raised blades. Directly behind them seven halftrack-mounted cannon moved spastically; roll forward, halt, fire, recoil; roll forward, halt, fire, recoil. Varina could hear the screaming projectiles cracking against the tower walls.

Behind the cannon conventional bulldozers, like courtiers laying a path for their king, smoothed the way for a massive boring machine.

Again and again the amber laser pulsed. Its light seemed to have little effect on the shields. The equipment kept on moving. When the laser beam raised to shoot over the lead bulldozers, it hit far down the canyon. She could tell by the screams that the human army was down there, still in the dark.

"It's beautiful," Alta said.

Varina watched the deadly beams of light, the star-

102

bursts of explosions, the fires that burned here and there, the backdrop of mountains and morning sky, and she had to admit it was.

They were sitting on the ground now just watching. It was the only thing they could do. Crossing the canyon was out of the question; to walk along the rim meant being exposed to light and being seen. So far the only evidence of life in the tower was the redirected laser fire.

There was a lull in the cannon barrage and then all seven fired at once. Sound waves reverberated off the canyon walls and re-echoed through the peaks. Varina saw the right side of the tower wall begin to crumble. Within moments there was a hum of aircars. Two were coming from the direction of Kelador and these were not fired on. Four smaller craft came hurrying in from the south. Too late, the tower realized they were enemy craft and were bombing. There was a great explosion that hurled the four watchers backward like tumbleweeds. When she could see again Varina saw the red beacon wink out. From the canyon below a great cheer went up as the light died.

Searchlights swept out from the aircars that had returned and hovered over the tower. In the beams, smoke and dust created a gray fog. Then, as the smoke drifted away, she heard Alta whisper, "Look!" and saw her point. "What is that?" Looking down at the tower base, she saw the drones and knew Sidra was aware of the war. These drones had to be released by palace controls. But why was war being allowed?

It was as if an ant hill had been violated. The drones were swarming up out of the ruined tower, pushing aside stone and masonry, jumping, slipping, sliding down into the canyon. Behind, through the break in the walls, more came boiling out, their bodies gleaming dusty gold from the lights overhead. The pilots, curious, came in for a closer look. A myriad of small beams shot up like ruby crystals to pierce the attackers. Jason counted four crashes before Cornelius shouted, "Duck!" as a craft out of control spun in low over their mesa and exploded a few miles back in the desert. In the wreckage died one of the two pilots still searching for Varina.

Their aerial enemies destroyed, the drones moved down the canyon like a flow of molten gold. As they ran, they sang a harsh, cruel hymn of death. The throbbing resonance of their song echoed and re-echoed from the canyon walls until it blotted out all their sound.

Directly below there was wild activity to get the bulldozers moving but separated so that the cannon could fire past their obstruction. But the drones moved too swiftly. They vaulted up over the bulldozer shields onto the engine hoods. Ruby beams shot out. Bodies were flung to the ground. One by one the tractors stopped but the drones kept on moving. With deadly efficiency they cleaned out the men on the cannon. The drivers on the bulldozers surrounding the boring machine had time and space to defend themselves, or make an attempt to do so. They ran at the drones full speed, blades half lifted. Some drones were cut in half on impact, others decapitated. But one by one the drivers died. The angry hum of death grew louder.

Its driver dead and slumped onto the control levers, the great miner crushed on, pushing bulldozers aside. A jolt switched on its reamers; their drill bits began to chew through boulders, bodies, and Delikon drones. The drones fanned out around the miner, their weapons no match for its massive armor. Like a blind monster it lurched ahead until the terrain aimed it against the canyon wall. The reamers screamed into the stone and the miner fed upon the rock until it died.

Beside her, Varina felt a shudder shake Jason's body. She studied first him, then Alta. Their faces were very pale, their eyes wide. They sat hugging their knees, watching the battle. She knew they could not see the drones clearly from this distance and she was grateful for that. For she could see them, and these defenders of Kelador frightened her. She moved over so that she could put an arm around each friend's shoulder, and all three felt comforted.

Leaving the miner to bury itself in the canyon wall, the drones swarmed down on the human army. Those in vehicles died in a ruby flash. Those on foot were more fortunate, for some had the sense to throw themselves on the ground and feign death. But most ran, and the drones followed.

"Cian!" Cornelius lifted her to her feet in one swift swoop and pointed down the cliff in front of them. Three drones were scaling the canyon wall, mounting from ledge to ledge, coming toward them, humming.

Twenty-two

EVEN IN THE SURGE of fear that flooded her, Varina had to admire her escort's coolness. But then he did not know any better.

"Release me." She spoke very softly. "We do not want them to think you are harming me. Step back slowly. Make no sudden sound or movement."

Cornelius let go of her, and she stepped in front of him. Her arms outstretched as if to protect the three behind her, she began to sing. To her friends the song was as strange as the language in which she sang it.

Three pairs of huge cinnamon eyes focused on her. There was no enmity, no recognition, no feeling. The humming stopped but the drones continued to climb. They topped the ledge and stood looming down above Varina, silent, listening to her song.

Except for those beautiful mad eyes it was hard to believe they were breathing creatures and not robots. Their faces had been simplified to an abstract in the ovoid head. Taller than the ambassadors, more golden and more heavily built, they looked immensely strong.

Their bodies shone like oiled metal. Their feet had been gridded for traction and studded with serrated nails. The outer edge of each "hand" was also a blade-sharp serration. On each "hand" a "finger" had been replaced by thorp lasers; she could see the power cell bulge in their thorax.

She paused, waiting for response to the ancient song of command of the High House. Then from their vocal chambers came resonant answer. "Your song is sacred," their deep tones said, "but your scent profane. Still, while profane, you do not flee us."

She could not be sure they would obey her, or even understand. They had been coded differently and long ago. She raised her left arm and pushed back the sleeve. "I wear the Seal of Privilege of the High House of D'laak."

"Yet you are deformed, debased."

She saw expression enter their eyes now, suspicion, confusion. And so, in desperation, she ordered them, "Touch me and know your superior." But as she sang the command she was not sure they would recognize her. If she had been human too long, in an instant she and her friends would die.

At her command they hesitated, then moved toward her with the oiled and brittle steps of scorpions. A golden arm extended, claws retracted, a padded fingertip touched her lips with respectful gentleness. Another touched the emerald stone; a third absorbed her breath. Behind her she heard Alta's breath hiss in a quick inhalation of fright and Cornelius's feet scuffled uneasily upon the stone. "Be still," she warned them. "Do not move or speak."

The drones stepped away and hummed among themselves. Varina sighed with relief to be still alive. They turned again toward her. "Child of the High House, you are long in exile," they sang as they saluted her. "Why are you here, so deformed, so far from the Ruling House of Kelador, so far from the Plains of D'laak?"

It was too involved to explain. "I serve as you do."

106

"We salute you. We will kill the aliens?"

"They are in my care."

"We must know them."

Varina nodded. "The drones are going to touch you," she told her three friends. "Do not be afraid; there is no pain. They do so that you may be recognized as friend."

One by one the drones advanced. Alta and Jason stood still as frightened rabbits, eyes downcast. But Cornelius turned his head away as the first hand reached toward him. Varina saw the revulsion in his face, and she knew that if he saw her as she was and would be, he would look at her in the same way.

"Be still, Cornelius," she said gently. "Endure it. It will save you from far greater indignity."

The warrior drones assimilated the minute secretions from the alien tissues, singularly and together. They sang when assimilation was completed, but the earthlings did not understand and heard only a sonorous hum. Like dancers, the drones moved back to the cliff's edge and were gone, jumping down from ledge to ledge as if rappelling on invisible ropes.

Cornelius sat down; his legs had given out beneath him. Alta and Jason joined him. "Look at my knees shake!" Jason whispered, and then giggled nervously. "Their fingers feel like a cat's tongue." Alta was fingering her lower lip where they had touched her and looking at Varina speculatively. She was going to say something, then looked over at Cornelius and changed her mind. Cornelius had not seen the ambassadors, and Alta had sworn not to mention them to anyone.

Cornelius was sitting in shock, staring off into the canyon. Varina knelt beside him and took his left hand in both of hers. His hands felt dry and rough and very cold. "I am sorry." She did not say for what. It would have taken too long and frightened him more.

"You went into those buildings where these things were kept?" Cornelius said. "You knew they looked like that?"

107

"Yes."

"You weren't afraid?"

"I was very much afraid."

"What if they had been alive in there. How could I have protected you?"

"They have been programmed . . ."

He looked at her. "Programmed? They *are* alive, aren't they?"

"Yes. But—"

"It doesn't matter, cian. I won't understand. No matter what you say. That there are such things in the world. That they are on *our* side, killing people. That this—" He gestured toward the chaos in the canyon and shook his head, at a loss to express what he felt.

"You have done all anyone could," she said. "Because of you we are all together and unharmed. By the end of the day we will be back in Kelador. We are tired now. . . ."

He nodded from habitual politeness but did not seem particularly interested.

"Do we have anything left to eat?" Jason asked, half apologetic for being hungry at a time like this.

"We are all probably hungry," agreed Varina, and felt a sense of relief at being able to do something so simple as rummage with him through their packs.

"You'll feel better," Alta said, offering Cornelius a bruised orange from her pack. He hesitated, then took it. He looked from one to the other. "This doesn't seem to bother you children the way it does me," he said wonderingly. "Am I getting old?"

"No," said Alta with a gentle smile, "but you could do with a bath." Then, seeing her fingers were leaving smudges on her orange, "So could I!"

The pass the boundary tower had filled was blocked by rubble, impossible for them to climb over. They would have to find another route into Kelador. When they had eaten they set off for the canyon, climbing down from ledge to ledge, slipping and sliding, grasping at bushes in crevices, helping each other over the bad spots.

A haze of smoke and dust hung over the canyon floor. It was so quiet now that the raucous cawing of crows startled them. The flies that were beginning to gather buzzed past in the stillness. Abandoned machinery was scattered about, some of it still burning. Black oily smoke and heat waves rose above it. Bodies lay where they had fallen, draped from machinery, arched over boulders, in the pale sand with arms akimbo, eyes at last looking straight into the sun.

Cornelius led them west along the canyon. In the first two miles they walked, they saw no living human or drone, and they quit looking at the dead. This was a mistake, for not all that seemed dead were safely so. As the quartet had climbed down into the canyon, they were watched, and when they walked away a man rose from the sand and followed, a hunter stalking prey.

Varina heard rock clink against rock and, turning, saw a soldier in a shabby blue uniform. He carried a rifle. As her eyes met his, she saw his face twist with such hatred that she cried out in a pitch beyond human hearing. Cornelius heard only her deep gasps for breath as she called again and again for help and heard from the west a distant answer.

Hatred was not within her understanding, but she had never seen such an ugly emotion expressed on a human face, and it frightened her as nothing else had. Then, to her added horror, Cornelius pushed past to stand between her and this danger. He would face this thing meant for her.

"Put down the gun!" He spoke as if to a frightened child. "What's wrong with you? Can't you see you are frightening the children?"

Varina expected to hear the rifle crack, but instead the other man answered.

"Don't try to stop me. She's no child. She's got the eyes!"

"She's my daughter. Stay back!" But the soldier kept coming.

"She's one of them and I am going to kill her. Maybe I can't do anything else, but I am going to kill her."

"You don't know what you're . . ." Cornelius started to say.

"Shut up!" he yelled without looking at him. "She's one of them! I saw those things go up to her! I lay there and saw it! Everyone else is dead, but she's still alive! Why is that? Why?" His voice cracked with rage, and Varina felt sick with his anger. Suddenly his eyes focused on something in the distance, and he squinted to see better.

Cornelius chose that moment to rush him. That too was a mistake. As soon as Cornelius moved the soldier fired point blank. Cornelius's rush carried him into the man and both fell. The soldier's arm struck a stone and the rifle went flying. Their bodies rolled together on the ground and both lay still.

It happened so fast that for an instant even Varina stood dumb-struck. Then she ran and knelt beside the two men and reached for Cornelius's outstretched hand. There was no pulse in the wrist or at the throat. The soldier groaned. She felt rather than saw Alta and Jason kneel beside her. Together they rolled Cornelius over onto his back. His eyes were open. Blood trickled from the corner of his mouth. In his face was the same stillness that lay all around them. She reached over and gently closed his eyes. In the stillness of her mind she was crying, Why is this allowed?

There was the sound of heavy running footsteps, and the three drones loomed above them, then another and another until seven in all stood encircling them. Alta and Jason did not look up but knelt beside Cornelius holding his hands, rubbing their warmth as if that could somehow change things.

Varina knew this could not be changed. "I am in need of aid and protection." At the sound of her voice Alta and Jason looked at her, numb. "You"—she pointed to one drone—"will make sure this alien never wakes." She pointed to the soldier. There was a "thorp!" of sound. Ruby light and gray ash were streaked down the still form of the soldier. "And you will hollow a crypt for a friend of the Ruling House." She pointed to the red sandstone wall of the canyon. Then, rising, she pulled Alta and Jason to their feet. "Come, let him be carried."

"Can they help him?" Alta asked wistfully.

Varina shook her head. "He is dead." Somehow saying the words seemed to make it so. Definite, unchangeable, emptiness where comfort had been. She closed her eyes, took a deep breath, and shut off that portion of her mind that registered feeling.

A drone knelt and lifted the big man in his arms as an adult would carry a sleeping child. Flanked by drones, the three children walked with them to the cliff face.

This cannot be, Varina thought. This is all a nightmare and we will wake and be safe in our own beds. And there will be a bath and breakfast and birds singing in the gardens. And why is that crow walking?

Drones formed a solid wall in front of them. She heard the repeated firing of lasers and felt a glow of heat around her ankles as the sandstone melted and fused with the photons' excitation.

It was a spacious crypt, lined in glassy smoothness. On its glowing floor the drones heaped clean sand and lay Cornelius upon its bed.

"Are we going to leave him here? Alone?" Jason was near the breaking point, and his question was almost more than Varina could bear. She took refuge in curtness.

"Yes. We are. As he would leave us. He is dead, Jason. Because he is dead we are still alive. We will not waste his death by indulging our grief, by staying here. He would not be so foolish." She saw Alta looking at her as if she had just seen a great flaw develop in Varina's character. It was difficult, but if she gave them one hint of sympathy, or let them know how she felt, she was afraid they would go helpless on her. There was no time for that now. "Say good-bye to him. We must go on."

They did so, both of them with streams of tears

111

running down their dirty faces. Then Varina stepped up to the hot glistening chamber and looked down at her one real human friend. From her wrist she took the Ring of Privilege. It was too big to fit his fingers and so she put it on his chest and folded his hands over it for safe-keeping. She sang him a song he would never hear and which she had heard long ago when a ruler of D'laak was entombed, and she told him good-bye and she left him.

The drones sealed the crypt with a flow of molten stone, and on its glistening surface she had them write:

HERE SLEEPS CORNELIUS
HOUSE FRIEND
POSSESSOR OF THE RING OF PRIVILEGE
OF THE
HIGH HOUSE OF D'LAAK

in a language no earthling could ever read.

Twenty-three

THE DRONES COULD DO no more. Varina sent them back to join their cohorts.

Alone now, the three children set off again, walking out of the canyon. Varina talked to keep them all from thinking. "Even if we could get up the canyon, we cannot climb up to the tower. So what we have to do now is find something we can drive. . . ."

"Can you drive?" asked Jason. He sounded like he didn't care much if she could or not.

"Not well," she said, "but it does not matter what I run over out here. We will find a car. . . ." She was blithering and she knew it. But she could not stop—

because if she stopped, she would see Cornelius's dead face.

When at last they found a vehicle still intact it was a truck tractor. Its big wheels were encircled with steel studs for off-road travel. Its cab doors hung open, and there was a small melt hole in the windshield, but, other than that, it seemed unharmed except for gouges in the brown paint. Varina climbed up the ladder into the cab, sat down in the driver's seat, and felt overwhelmed by the completeness of her ignorance.

But being helpless was not going to get them anywhere. If only Cornelius were here, he would know what to do. Thinking about what he would do helped. Cornelius was very methodical. She checked the control panel; many buttons had pictures on them. The layout wasn't so different from that of other vehicles she'd ridden in for so long. That was the ignition, there were the gears, there were the trailer hitch, brakes, lights. After the minutes of study, she pressed an ignition button and the wheel motors came on, along with a glowing row of buttons that encouraged her immensely. The dial showed the power cells still fully charged and adequate for a long trip. She pressed the release button for the trailer and heard it hiss free.

"Come on," she called down to Alta and Jason. They stared up at her, not sure they should trust themselves to this new danger. She climbed down and almost pushed them up the ladder into the cab and saw them get into the back seat. There they stretched out, their feet on the bench seat between them. She wasn't sure if they were displeased with her or merely looking for comfort.

All of them were quiet as she put the truck into gear, moved carefully out in a U-turn, and rumbled west out of the canyon. She was absorbed in steering, avoiding the abandoned machinery and the dead.

There was too much she could not understand. Much of the attack had taken place in daylight. Yet aside from the drones and the tower's lasers, Kelador had made no defense. She had not seen one single monitor plane come over. And the craft that bombed the tower appeared to come from Kelador's side of the border. Her belief in Kelador's ability to defend itself was shaken, and she did not want to think too deeply about why that might be.

At the western end of the canyon Varina turned southeast. A pink dust trail rose behind them as the tractor cut across the dry land. Evidence of stripmining was everywhere; mountains turned into a rutted jumble of hills cut by rivulets of erosion through the red earth. Scrub and marsh grasses grew in some of the depressions, but there were no birds. Occasionally they would see people, refugees hiding beside what available water they could find. The people fled as the tractor approached.

When they reached the strip blackened by laser fire, Varina turned back toward the mountains, and the land grew green again. Because she had been preoccupied by driving, she felt better. She wasn't sure about Alta and Jason. They remained so quiet that often during the day she had thought they were asleep, only to find them staring wide-eyed out the window, sometimes with tears running down their faces.

By dusk they passed the old roadbed that led to the tunnels. It had been heavily trafficked, but they saw no one else now. When Varina stopped to look more closely at the wheeltracks and ruts, she thought she understood why. The ground was thick with the footprints of drones. They had come from Kelador into sector nine.

When, five days before, they had looked down from the tunnel windows, the valley floor had been pristine, unmarred by man for centuries. No longer. The road gashed through the woods, trees were uprooted and burned, temporary fords had been bulldozed through the meandering streams. No tower was visible from down here.

"Does that mean they've crossed the boundary here, too?" Alta said, looking at the destruction.

"Thinking about that will not help us," Varina said.

114

"Now we will think about getting through tonight. In the morning, we will think about getting through the day. And by this time tomorrow night, we will be eating dinner at the palace."

"Will we?" Jason spoke for the first time in hours.

"If we can get as far as the path to the sanctuary, yes."

"And if we can't?" said Alta.

"Then we will have a very late dinner."

She was afraid to turn on the headlights and, when it got too dark to see, pulled off under the trees and stopped for the night. "We will sleep here," she said. "Shall we get out and stretch our legs?"

In the dark outside the truck cab, if she shut off her mind, it was easy to believe nothing had changed. The pines smelled sweet; the night wind moved through the treetops. Overhead the stars shone unchanged. She walked a little way from the others and leaned against a tree to look up at the orderly stars.

Thoughts were not flowing logically any more—only emotions. I am like Alta and Jason, she admitted to herself. I am tired and afraid and I want to go home. Having admitted that, she felt a new surge of sympathy for the others. She was at least comparatively safe; they were aliens to both camps now.

In the eastern sky, a streak of light caught her attention. It was a shooting star. Or was it? Very high and moving higher out into space. It seemed to touch a larger star and merge with it. Then, to her horror, the greater star flared green and moved off.

"The ambassadors' ship is leaving!" Her cry was inaudible, an exhalation of despair. "They are leaving!" She had never known such disappointment and, added to the grief she already bore, it stunned her so she nearly doubled over in pain. When she searched the sky again, there, farther out but still identifiable, was the green band of ion-glow of a starship heading past Orion.

· There was no need to hurry now; today, tomorrow, three days from now—it would make little difference.

She had ten more earth years. The rush to return to Kelador had all been for nothing. The ship was leaving ahead of schedule. Leaving her behind. But why? Why would they leave now? She tried to think of a reason that suggested something other than things she didn't even want to consider—maybe the Ruling House had been attacked; maybe Sidra—and control the grief that came over her in waves.

"Are you ill?" Jason was holding her shoulders and peering into her face. "Say something, Varina, please!" he begged. "Are you ill?"

"No." Her voice was slurred, and fuzzy. "No. Why?"

He didn't answer for a moment but he put his hand on her forehead, checking for a fever. His hands felt cold and clammy.

"You were looking up at the sky and moaning," he told her. "Deep in your throat. We thought—we didn't know what."

"Were you crying, Varina?" Alta said.

"I—no—I was not crying."

"Were you singing?" Jason persisted.

"Yes," Varina lied. "I guess I was; it's an old, old song to the stars." She felt Jason's grip tighten on her arm and was ashamed. They were more lost and frightened than she, and by her lack of self-discipline she was scaring them more. "I am all right," she assured them, "really I am. I am sorry to scare you. I guess I was half asleep and dreaming. . . ."

Alta gave a sigh, apparently unsatisfied with that. "Why don't you just admit you were crying?" she said. "Come, let's eat."

They ate dry protein biscuits and mushy apples, sitting on the ground, leaning against the truck wheels. No one talked. It was chilly now that night had fallen. The warmth from the cooling wheel motors felt good on their backs. Except for occasional breezes moving the treetops, the night was still—too still. No insects

116

sang. No bird cried out in its dreams. No animals moved in the bushes.

"I think we had better sleep in the tractor," Varina said. She got no arguments.

"One of us should stay awake and guard," said Jason.

"We should," she agreed, "but, tired as we are, none of us will stay awake. We will lock the door."

Twenty-four

AFTER THE CLEAN AIR outside, the closed truck cab smelled of grease and dust. But it was warm. Alta and Jason stretched out on the bench seat and immediately fell into an unmoving sleep, punctuated by snores of exhaustion.

Varina sat alone, across from the driver's seat, and felt isolated from them and the whole world. She slumped in the corner, head back, watching the stars through the window, thinking, wondering how all this had happened. How, in less than a week, had her world fallen apart? Didn't Sidra know what was happening? Or Vashlin—or any of them? And why had no one looked for them? Didn't Sidra care about her either? But then, Varina reminded herself, she was only one tiny part of the whole order, her companions only human. Logically she could accept this. But she had been emotionally contaminated by too long exposure to those humans. And she hurt.

She was unaware of falling asleep, yet she must have for she became conscious of dreaming. In the dream she was trapped in a glass box. Outside something was hunting her. It made a noise . . . outside. She woke, suddenly sure it was no dream, afraid to move. The relaxed breathing of her friends reassured her for a moment; they were safely asleep.

There was a sharp creak and the tractor cab rocked. Without moving she opened her eyes slightly and peered under the lids. There was a large darkness against the window; she opened her eyes wider to see. Looking in from the other side of the glass, only inches away, was the open-mouthed face of a drone. She nearly quit breathing.

The chassis rocked again and a second head rose up beside the first. She could hear claws scrape to cling to the dew-slick metal of the roof. Then one of them tried the door. The cab shook. With everything in her she wanted to reach over and make sure the lock-pin was pressed down but she knew if she moved the cab would be laser-lighted in an instant. And then they spoke.

"Aliens?" The notes sounded like a bullfrog.

"Aliens."

"Dead?"

"Unknown."

"Kill?"

"Listen." The faces turned away from the window toward the cliff side beyond, where the tunnels were.

For what? In spite of her fear, Varina found herself listening, straining to hear what they heard. But all she could hear was her pulse pounding in her head. Behind her, Alta sighed and moved in her sleep. If she woke and said anything . . . or sat up quickly . . . But if Varina reached out to warn and they saw her movement . . . While she was debating it, the drones suddenly let go and dropped to the ground. Sprung from their weight, the cab rocked again.

"What is it?"

"Sh-h-h-h." She prayed only Jason would hear her.

"What is it?" he repeated in the faintest whisper.

"Drones. Sh-h-h-h."

From far across the valley came a soft flutelike call, followed by a throbbing bass tone. When the last of the bass notes stopped echoing, one of the drones beside the truck gave answer in ascending tonal whoops so resonant that Varina felt her mind being invaded

118

by circles of sound. She had never heard them sing for pleasure in the wind of this world, never heard the music chain echo from the mountain sides. It was as beautiful as it was frightening.

The flutelike call came again, nearer, and again the cascade to low tones. From outside she heard heavy footsteps moving away at a run, and both the runners answered now in a whooping song of mindless joy. The glass in the cab hummed in vibrant response as the sound waves bounced off its surface. Inside the cab all sound seemed to have stopped. When she felt it was safe to risk it, Varina slid up in her seat and looked out.

"Where have they gone?" Jason whispered.

"To join the others."

"Varina?" It was Alta's voice, and it was terrified.

"It is all right," Varina whispered. "I am here. We are all safe."

"I'm scared."

"I know. But it is only singing. Jason, were you awake?"

"I woke up when they rattled the door. I was afraid to move."

"Good boy."

"How did we live through that, Varina?" wondered Alta. "Can they smell us through the door?"

"No. They were scouts; I think they decided we were dead."

"Will they come back?"

"Those two? Probably not."

"Others?"

"Look!" Jason whispered. "Up there where the lights are!"

And then Varina saw something she remembered for as long as she lived. In the windowed mountain walls high above the trees, great half-ovals of red light began to appear, progressing around the mountain like a deadly train. Something was coming through the ancient tunnels out of Kelador. She dared to lower the window and listen.

119

The last drones of Kelador were marching to war and, as drones did, these sang. They sang a chant of jubilance at release from their long sleep. They sang a chant of longing for the battles to come. They had been given no promise of paradise but only the passion to kill, and their passion was pure and gave them great joy.

That was the song Varina heard. What her friends heard was quite different. If one could hear the sound of death moving in the night and see the lamps it carried, then what they heard and saw was heavy-booted death. It poured through the tunnels and also below, crossing the valley, out of the night, under the stars, hurrying to the west. And as it marched it sang a hymn so strange that they felt lost and alien in their own world.

Twenty-five

As SIDRA WALKED in the garden, the tigers coughed. On the other side of the moat one of them paced with her, his eyes never leaving her face. When she stopped, he stopped. And watched. When she walked on, he would crouch and then, on velvet feet, stalk her.

The beauty of him in the night, light on shadow, rippling and blending . . . She would miss these creatures—as she would miss the stillness of earth's nights, the small part of earth she knew. And in a way she would miss even the solitude. And that surprised her.

"Have I had time to adapt to confinement, then?" she wondered aloud to the tiger. "Will I be as vulnerable outside this prison as you would be outside yours?"

The tiger made no answer but to twitch the tip of his tail. "Wise creature." She commended him.

Three of the pilots had not returned. Shot down by boundary lasers . . . captured towers controlled by men from sector nine. The thought of the wasted lives haunted her. Was that what had happened to Varina? Did she too die in her last week of service to this backward planet? Sidra did not want to believe that. They had searched and found no trace of her. No bodies, no graves. Perhaps the escort was frightened for her and the companions; perhaps he had hidden them for safety.

But Varina would come back. She was a child of the High House—a child who wore the Ring of Privilege. If she was alive, she would come back. If she returned and found them gone, found herself trapped in alien form to live her life long on an alien planet . . . At the thought of such loneliness Sidra moaned aloud in agony. The tigers fell silent in fear.

"Who's there?" A guard's frightened voice called. "Who's there?" Lights hidden in the shrubbery flashed on and made holes in the night. A guard came running, gun drawn, and, seeing her, stumbled to a halt. "Madam?" His voice cracked. "Did you—are you safe?"

She could hear other guards hurrying in their direction. So little gravity, such heavy feet.

"I am quite safe, sentry."

He gave a hesitant smile and an equally imprecise salute in his discomposure. "I'm sorry, t'kỹna. Some of the sounds of these animals make my hair stand on end."

"Thank you for your concern, corporal. Now please tell your comrades to turn out the lights. Good night."

She nearly smiled at his awkwardness; there was something endearing about him. The lights went off but her mood had been broken. "Aron will determine your fate, my friends," she told the tigers. "As, in a way, he has influenced mine. If it were possible, I would free you. But you would kill, and I would be your first victim. You are more direct than your fellow creatures."

121

There was time for a last walk around the reflecting pools, and she stood looking down at the stars mirrored in the water's surface. The restructuring could be put off no longer. She crossed the bridge to the largest of the temple buildings.

Vashlin was waiting for her in the anteroom to the surgery. It had been so long since she had seen his true form that she had to look twice to recognize him. He apparently gave the matter no thought, his mind on other issues.

"You are the last of us . . ."

"But one . . ."

". . . and it may already be too late. The shuttle viewer reports intense fighting all along sector nine's borders. The drones cannot protect the towers, but they seem to be holding the intruders back."

"How long?"

"That depends on how effectively humans can kill drones. Or on their air power. They are using modified aircars to bomb the towers."

"And if they can cross the mountains with them?"

"They may bomb the palace."

"We are ready for you now, madam," a surgical technician called. Sidra waved them off.

"We should leave." She spoke as if to herself. "You should leave . . ." and it all became clear. "It is foolish to waste time now with surface cars to spare human sensibilities. Summon the shuttle craft here to the palace. It can land in the rock garden. The human staff will be terrified, but it scarcely matters now what they see. If the guards attack us, kill if you must. I want no more Delikon lost!"

"It will take five days for you to complete restructuring," Vashlin reminded her. "We may not have that much time. You can travel in your present alien form."

"Encapsulated like a drone? And experience black nothingness all the way home? Disembark looking like this?" She gave a human shudder.

"Once you enter the restructuring chamber we cannot leave until the process is complete. The equipment is too heavy and too sensitive to place on board the shuttlecraft. I think there is time enough, but I hesitate to gamble with your life."

"That is a chance I will take, Vashlin. You alone will be in command while I am in process. If it becomes necessary to flee, which I doubt, you are to board and leave. Better one of us than all."

"But what would you do if you stepped out of the cylinder to find us gone—and humans in control of Kelador?"

"I would have no choice."

"But you are t'kyna. The House would be bereft."

"The House would survive. It would choose a new head."

"You are part of us. We forget that here, in this lonely world of one-by-one, trapped inside soft skins, sensorially deprived. . . ."

"It is the function of our House to serve the High House as colonial administrators. So it has been; so it will be. We are the stewards and also—I am the guardian."

"But Kiru . . ."

"Vashlin, if waiting for me jeopardized our final departure, you are to leave. One more thing; if Varina is found . . ."

"It is too late, t'kyna. Too late . . ."

"If she *is* found, then we will wait until she can be brought here—if we must kill every human in Kelador to do it! Is that understood?"

"Kiru's final orders were for your welfare."

"Kiru spoke more from affection than true understanding. If you must, you will leave me." She looked deep into the eyes of the creature who had shared her exile. "And I will know your grief and feel regret that I have caused you pain."

"T'kyna?" the Delikon technician said pleadingly.

"Coming. You will not allow our House to suffer any more losses because of me, Vashlin. Swear that you will not."

The great eyes closed as if in pain, the head bowed.

123

Then slowly, with infinite regret, "I swear that to you, t'kyna."

She reached out and touched his arm in passing, and entered into surgery. In a few moments came merciful oblivion. By the time the sun's first rays streamed into the highest windows of the Great Hall, she floated vertically and gravity free within a crystal cylinder. Her level of awareness was not outward but deep, deep within as her body fought the trauma of this metamorphosis that was restructuring. Within the plasma all was dark wet silence, except for that one brief moment at sunrise when light first pierced her with pain. She was aware yet unaware of the cells' biochemical alterings. And in that drug-induced state, she felt dread and fear—that she would awake to find herself alone upon this world, as vulnerable as a caged tiger.

Twenty-six

IT WAS RAINING when they left in the morning. Low clouds hung thick over the mountains. The windshield wiper swept half circles of clarity ahead and pushed water through the hole in the windshield to run over the dashboard and drip on the floor.

Like creatures from a nightmare the army of drones was gone by first light. They left desolation behind them. Laser-cut trees lay everywhere, their boughs limp and dull in the rain. The grass that had carpeted the valley floor was crushed and black with burning, the stream full of muddy foam.

Varina had started up the tractor and pulled out as soon as it was light enough to see. Alta and Jason were still asleep, their eyelids twitching as uneasy dreams passed through their minds. In the entire tractor cab the only thing Varina found comforting was the warm glow of buttons on the control panel. The longer she could see them, the sooner she would get home.

They traveled east, always uphill, and the farther they went, the narrower the valley became, until the mountains hemmed them in on both sides. Aron's men had been working here. A big slash of crude new road cut through the end of one mountain and angled up around the next.

The rain was turning this primary road of clay and gravel to liquid mud and loose stone. The steel-studded wheels of the tractor found little that was firm to grip. Only its weight gave the big vehicle enough traction to move.

Since the tractor had independent suspension and drive on each set of wheels, an experienced driver would have had little trouble even now. But Varina was not an experienced driver of anything. Nor was her mind as alert as it should have been. When the road became a steep shelf along the edge of the mountain, with solid rock to the right, a thousand-foot drop-off to the left, and a slippery surface beneath her, she was in trouble.

Faced with the incline and loss of traction, and not properly geared down, the motors began to labor. As they crept around a curve, the rear end of the tractor skated with sickening ease. Varina felt her stomach clutch itself in fear.

From the driver's side she could look down from the high cab into the canyon below. It was a long way down. She wished she had not looked, and clutched the wheel tighter as if to hold on to it. Sitting half up-right, jaws clenched, she was unaware of anything else moving but her eyes as she looked from road's edge to control panel to rear-view mirrors. Then her right arm seemed hindered, and she glanced over. Sitting next to her, as close as they could get for comfort, were Alta and Jason. They were very much awake.

"Hi," said Alta and gave her a weak smile.

"Do you think we should walk?" Varina asked as she hauled the tractor carefully around a curve.

"I'd feel safer," said Jason, "but it would take us forever. Can we make it up here?"

"We can try," Varina said slowly. "Unlock the door on your side and keep your hand on the latch. If we start to roll over, there will be little time to get out."

She could hear Jason doing as he was told, but the two of them didn't speak again for minutes.

Up and up they crept around the mountain, the road seeming to get worse with each yard they traveled. When they were high enough to be above a nearby peak, the unobstructed wind smashed against the tractor in gusts that shook it. Rain blew so wildly the windshield wiper could not clear it away fast enough. Twice the wind lifted the wiper arm from the pane and nearly wrenched it off. It was then Varina began to pray.

With each wind buffeting she was sure she would lose control of the wheel and they would go over. She wanted to get out and run; she knew she would be safe. But Alta and Jason would not be. Once they were out of the protection of this motorized metal box, the wind might push them over. The rain would chill them. They could not run as she could. She was aware that her legs were shaking, and it occurred to her then that perhaps even she could not run fast enough.

Around another curve, and then came a straight stretch where the road left this mountain to cross a ridge over to the next. While still in the lee of this mountain, she stopped to rest and look out over the peaks and flex her nerve-cramped muscles. Over the hum of the idling motors the rain slashed against the cab; water ran off the wall beside them and poured over the road.

At one point behind them she saw a damaged boundary tower before clouds obscured it again. Its distance surprised her; she hadn't realized they had come so far. How had Aron's people made this road so quickly, so far into Kelador, without being stopped?

And where were they now? Headed toward the palace? Or had the road builders gone back to lead the others in?

"I—uh—I think we're sliding sideways," Jason said in choked tones. She didn't wait to see if she agreed, but moved the tractor into gear and inched away. Once they were out on the straightaway, there was nothing to stop the wind. It howled and gusted around them. Although they crossed in less than ten minutes, it seemed like forever to Varina, and when they reached the other side she wanted to stop and shake awhile. But there was no safe place to stop.

She drove on because she had no choice. The road became a mere slash out of the mountain, with no grading, no leveling, no banking, but, oddly enough, easier for the wheels to sink into. And sink in they did in this rain. The speed slowed to the pace of a human walk. In the rear-view mirror, Varina could see their tracks become twin rivers gleaming under the gray clouds.

"Look down there!" Jason pointed, and Varina glanced down. A big bulldozer lay halfway down the mountainside, its treads in the air, like an overturned beetle. A little farther on was the wreck of a huge tractor and the earth-mover it had pulled. Then Varina saw something on the road ahead, lying discarded in a pile against the cliff wall. The drones had come this way. She said nothing as she realized what it was, not even when Alta said, "Dead people!"

Ahead was more of the same, ruined equipment and ruined bodies. After the initial shock, Varina hardly bothered to look. It was regrettable, but it was done and could not be changed. She was far more bothered by the fact that the end of the road was in view and the tractor could hardly churn its way through the mud beneath them now. They were going to have to walk; they had no choice, and she told Alta and Jason so.

"How far do you think it is to the sanctuary?" said Jason. "Can we make it?"

"We have to," she reminded him. "By aircar, five miles. On foot, all day—if we can find the route from here."

"What if we can't?" said Alta.

"We will." She steered the tractor over against the cliff wall. An avalanche ahead had brought down enough loose stone and earth to block the way. "Put on as much as you can comfortably wear," she said. "It is easier to wear than carry." She shut off the motors and sat for a moment, exhausted. The rain fingered the roof and blew off the hood in rivulets. The machine creaked as its weight settled into the mud. She put on the brakes automatically. "Come on. It may not be safe to sit here." She pulled herself rather stiffly to her knees, leaned over the seat back, and got her pack.

"I'm going to miss this truck," said Jason.

"I'm not," Alta said firmly. "I hate it and everything it represents."

Thinking about what it represented was a mistake for Varina, for it entailed remembering Aron and Aron's people, capture, and Cornelius. And all because she had failed. The Delikon had failed. She willed herself to stop. It could not be changed. Now she had to get home—and to get Alta and Jason home. "Come."

It was hard to keep the cab door open long enough for them all to get out. Encumbered by capes and packs, they struggled to climb down the ladder onto the narrow strip of mud. And no sooner were they all down than a gust of wind slammed the door shut. Varina led them off and did not look back.

On foot it was easy to see the drones had been here. Their tracks were everywhere, water-filled depressions that pocked the ground. The road builders had made camp in a canyon some fifty yards ahead. Only the charred remains of that camp stood now. What could burn on their machines was burned. Great lumps of fused and twisted metal remained. Varina took satis-

128

faction in knowing Aron had gone no farther on this road.

She hurried them past the wreckage and on down the mountain. They walked wherever the walking was easiest, heads down, rain splashing onto their capes, their leather boots soaked and sloshing.

The rain stopped, and by midafternoon they realized where they were. They had ridden through here less than a week before. Riding, singing in sunshine. If there was still wildlife here now, alive, it did not show itself. The only animals they saw were dead, their fur ash-streaked by lasers.

"It is not far now," Varina said to encourage them, and it wasn't—not compared to where they had started from. "About a mile ahead we should find the trail up to the sanctuary. From there on, it will be easy."

"Are we going up there again?" Jason asked, with the first enthusiasm he'd shown in hours.

"No. We will go to the stables by the landing pad. They can call an aircar for us . . ."

"If it's still there," said Jason.

She had not thought of that; she didn't know why. The stables had always been there, in her mind always would be there.

But they were not. The three came out of the woods just at dusk and crossed the landing pad. In the dim light Alta and Jason did not at first see what was there. But Varina did. Where houses and stables had stood, blackened trees lifted skeletal branches around char-filled cellar holes.

"Why?" she said aloud. "Why?"

"Why what?"

She pointed, unable to talk. By this time all three wanted to sit down and cry away the last of their energy. She couldn't even do that, but Alta and Jason could and they did. She stood beside them alone, helpless to comfort them or herself.

"Who is it? Who is there?" The voice was not friendly and it was frighteningly close, but the trio was so tired they no longer cared. None of them realized they were hearing Keladorian speech.

"These are the companions, Alta and Jason. I am the cian, Varina. Identify yourself."

There was noise in the bushes to their left and a man with white hair appeared. He advanced until Varina could see him. "I cannot see you in the dark. If you are the cian, you will know me."

"Keeper!"

"Cian! We thought— Where have you been? Where is your escort?"

"Cornelius is dead," she said simply. Then, remembering, "Why are you here?"

"It is a long story, cian, as I am sure yours is." He hurried forward as if to embrace her in his happiness to see her again. "My family will be so happy to see you. We will go . . ."

She slipped away from his outstretched arms. "Why are you here, keeper? Why have you left the sanctuary?"

She saw the smile fade from his face, but even then she never expected what he told her next. "The sanctuary is destroyed, cian," he said quietly. "The caves have been sealed. By the t'kyna's order."

She felt her mouth fall open, and suddenly the atmosphere of this planet was not adequate. She could hear herself gasping for air. Her last conscious thought was, "Then Sidra is dead."

Twenty-seven

THAT NIGHT as Varina slept, the people of Kelador saw the last of the great meteors arc across their sky. This one seemed a particularly bad omen, appearing as it did to rise directly from the palace.

Varina had not regained consciousness but instead

130

went from a period of what appeared to be near death into deep sleep. It was not a natural sleep and the keeper and his family watched over her through the night.

When she had collapsed, at the keepers' call for help, the other refugees from the sanctuary came out of hiding. They took the children to their makeshift camp, wrapped Varina tenderly in warm robes, and fed Alta and Jason.

"*Is* the t'kyna dead?" Alta asked.

"I spoke to her only two days ago," the keeper reassured them. But he did not say that he had seen the gatekeeper enter the caves, after also speaking to the t'kyna, and seal the doors behind him, forever. Nor did he answer Jason's questions as to who had burned this way station. "The t'kyna promised we would be flown to the palace from this point. She always keeps her word. She was very worried about you all. Your safe return will please her!"

Varina woke from a dream of floating under water, of seeing the sun rippling through the waves overhead. She remembered where she was and did not care. She could hear whispering, feel blankets rubbing her chin. She lay still, feeling her lens apertures open and close in response to sunlight through the windblown branches above her sleeping place. It was a mindless exercise, much better than thought.

Then came a sound that made her sit up. Aircars! Around her the people from the sanctuary began cheering, and hurrying into the clearing. She stood up, throwing blankets to a mound about her feet. Skimming over the hills below came five green aircars bearing the seal of the Ruling House. They approached slowly, cautiously, as if afraid of attack.

She had never seen so welcome a sight. Beside her Alta and Jason were speaking. She heard only the first thing they said—that Sidra was alive. Within five minutes the three of them, along with the keeper and his daughter, were in the first car and en route to the palace.

131

It seemed to Varina that the trip took forever. She did not talk but stared out the window at the scenery below. The peaceful villages, the lush green of Kelador seemed unreal after the country they had left behind. Then, in the distance, the roofs of the palace and temple enclave rose gleaming in the sun, peaceful and untouched.

They had no sooner set down than she was out running across the drive and up the steps. People came hurrying toward her. She dismissed their welcome. "Where's the t'kyna?"

"She went to the temple. . . ."

She waited to hear no more. Through the gardens, over the footbridge and up the hill, she went running as if chased by demons.

The guard on the footbridge stared after her. The last time he had seen her she was running like that. Then he had thought little of it, but now he appeared to be wondering if she had known something then that the rest of them did not, and what she knew now.

Seeing a girl in shabby common garb come racing up the hill, guards moved forward to stop her before they recognized her. She never even saw them but ran past and up the steps of the Great Temple. The doors were closed.

"You can't get in that way, cian," a guard called. "It has been shut ever since you left. Go around to the t'kyna entrance."

She went across the courtyard garden to Sidra's quarters. The door was locked, and so no servant responded to her call. She could not wait but pressed the secret lock release. The door did not open. It was under permanent seal.

"Sidra! Where are you?" The fear was coming back. "Sidra?"

"Cian?" A servant emerged from the staff quarters next door. "Cian! I wouldn't have recognized you. We had almost given up hope. . . ."

"Where is she?" Varina demanded to know.

The woman fell silent, and over her face came a

look of unease. "I'm not sure." She spoke hesitantly. "They've disappeared. . . . So many have gone. . . . Strange creatures were here. . . ."

"Where is the t'kyna?"

"She went into the temple last night—no, two nights ago. She hasn't come out. No one knows quite what to do . . ." Her voice trailed off. "We hoped you'd come back. You would know . . ."

Varina stared at her. The woman seemed bewildered.

"About what?"

"I'm not sure. Ever since the ship landed in the garden and those creatures came out of the temple. I saw them, you know. Great ugly things with heads like balls . . ."—she shivered—"like I don't know what. They say they've been seen elsewhere, you know. That they came from . . ." Her eyes were getting wilder and her voice higher.

"Stop it!" Varina ordered. "What about Sidra?"

"She went in there—where they were! And she didn't come back. And the next day—last night—the creatures came out of the temple and left in the ship. It glowed like a star. She didn't come back! She's still in there!"

"Have you seen her?"

"No! Oh, no! I won't go in there! They . . ." Hysteria shook the woman convulsively. "Don't go in there! Oh, please, don't—"

Varina left her there in the garden and ran down the tile-roofed walk to the t'kyna's private entrance to the temple. "Two days ago they saw her, spoke with her. Even if the shuttlecraft left from here, she did not go with them." And then she realized what she was saying. She had seen no other Delikon since she had arrived. Only humans. The pilots were human. The keeper, human. Where was the gatekeeper? "The creatures came out of the temple," she remembered Malote saying. Varina had thought of drones, not the entire Delikon staff. As it must have been. But two days ago? They had seen Sidra in human

133

form. Restructuring took at least five days; she was almost sure of that.

"Sidra?" She pressed open the security buttons. "Sidra?"

The small antechamber was empty but there was a mechanical sound from a wall speaker as a voice-activated recorder came on.

"Varina. I am grateful that you live." A videocom tape began to play back. "When you hear this . . ."

When she had heard it all and when the door that led to the temple proper slid open, Varina knew what she was going to see. One of the cylindrical columns would still be occupied. It was. The seventh from the end.

"Never wish for what should not be. It might happen." A woman had told Varina that once long ago. It had always seemed a silly maxim, no more. She had wished to stay on earth. Her wish had been granted.

There was pounding on the outer door. "Varina? Are you there? Let us in!" It was Alta and Jason, and with them she could hear adult voices. "If she doesn't come out, we'll break in and see what's going on in there."

She closed the door to the great Hall and locked it, turned off the videocom, and then opened the door to the garden. Alta grabbed her by the arm. "Are you okay?" she asked. Varina nodded. The keeper, some guards, and Malote were trying to see past her into the room. She put her hand on the plate, and the door slid shut behind her. Only Ruling House chemistry released these temple doors.

"The t'kyna is in the temple," she announced. "I am to join her there to give her a full report of our trip—when I am properly dressed," she added for Alta and Jason's benefit. "So shall we go bathe and . . ."

"And get some decent food?" said Jason as she took his hand. She nodded agreement.

"Cian." The guard commander stepped in front of her. "The staff, the others? Where are they?"

"They are in the temple." She lied without a moment's hesitation and then looked up at him as if she had just noticed his presence. She let go of her friends' hands. "What are you doing on temple grounds, officer?" The years of habit were her ally. Her kind had always been obeyed. The man hesitated. "What are your orders?" she continued.

"But that was before . . ."

"Your orders?"

"To keep everyone away from here."

"Very well. Do that," she told him. "If the t'kyna wishes that order changed, you will be told." She turned to her friends. "Shall we go? I have to hurry back here. Oh, keeper? The t'kyna welcomes you and your staff and hopes that you will be comfortable. A guest suite has been made ready for you. . . ."

And she walked off down the slope chatting and gave an inward sigh of relief to hear the others following—not satisfied, but trusting her.

What might happen here seemed minor to her now, compared to what was happening within that restructuring chamber. Kelador could be invaded, the palace could fall down—so long as the Great Hall was not entered until that chamber released Sidra.

Twenty-eight

IT WAS EARLY EVENING when Varina returned to the temple. The trees cast long shadows over the golden-green lawn. The air was crisp with the smell of autumn, chrysanthemums, and freshly cut grass. A white peacock saw her pass in her white and gold uniform and screamed in jealousy. His mad cry was answered by three others. In the pines the sparrows hushed their evening squabble to listen. From the distance came the sounds of an aircar coming from Vale, the clink of dinner preparation from the main kitchen, tigers roaring for meat. The snow on the mountain tops to the east gleamed gold, and beneath the fir line was the added gold of autumn hardwoods. Varina walked slowly, savoring it all.

"Cian." The guard at the bridge saluted, and she bowed her head in acknowledgment.

"I will be with the t'kyna until dawn. Perhaps longer," she told him. "We are not to be disturbed," and it was his turn to bow.

The wind over the water was cool. She shivered and walked a little faster.

In the temple all was still, warm and empty. As she crossed the floor, her boots noiseless on the thick carpet, the great room was already dim. The blue liquid within chamber seven looked black. She stood for a long time in front of that cylinder before she could bring herself to reach out and touch it. It was smooth and warm as a living thing, and it pulsed with the force of hidden pumps. She put her cheek against the warmth.

"I am back." Her voice was a whisper in the vast space. "I know you cannot really hear me now . . . but I must tell you. When you come out there may not be time . . . and you may not wish to hear me. It is almost over now . . . I want to go home . . ."

She rambled on, her thoughts disjointed, her voice a whispering sibilance in the still room. Night fell, and automatic timers turned on dim lights high overhead to keylight the spiral nebula. Still she talked on, pouring out all that had happened in the time she had been away—all the fear, all the sorrow, all the feelings of failure. Then, finally, in fatigue, it was over and she slumped to the carpet in front of the chamber and fell into deep sleep. She dreamed it was over and they were home and safe and whole.

When she woke the first thing she saw was morning light gleaming through the cylinder above her. During the night the color of the liquid had changed from deep blue to ultramarine. Within it was suspended a large and almost transparent form intricately traced with veins. As she watched, the sun pierced through a high window and struck the cylinder. For an instant a mysterious point of light gleamed from where an eye might be. The form writhed once within its cylinder and then was still again.

In the next two days, Varina broke her vigil only to eat and to change her clothing. When, briefly, she appeared in the palace, Alta and Jason found her strange and withdrawn, not listening to any of the exciting news they told her, having nothing to say to them. She would go to her suite, shutting them out, and re-emerge only to return to the temple. The truth was that she was scarcely aware of them or anyone else.

She did not hear them say that Aron had arrived "right after we did," had simply driven up to the palace and, finding no government in command, placed himself in charge. Because the people of Kelador made no resistance, he had brought few troops within its borders. After listening to the stories told by the remaining palace staff, he had hurried off to the north by aircar convoy. And, what pleased them most, he had told them they did not have to go to the academy. But none of this had any reality for Varina. Nothing outside the temple mattered now.

With each hour the form within the cylinder grew more distinct, more opaque. As the liquid changed from blue to green to amber, a shape of great power grew and filled the space until it seemed its force would break the walls. Each dawn the pinpoint of light appeared at the top of the cylinder. Always oriented toward the east, it would glow and disappear, and the creature within felt pain.

Before dawn on the morning of the third day of her vigil, Varina was wakened by an insistent bell tone. A computerized voice was murmuring from hidden speakers. "Those in terrestrial form must equip themselves with protective breathing devices. Atmosphere will begin to alter in ten earth minutes. At that time all exits will airlock. Those in terrestrial form . . ."

She got up groggily from the carpet and hurried to the lab next to Sidra's office, where the last few bubble helmets were stored. Helmet on, she returned to watch. These last minutes seemed longer than all the hours gone before.

Sounds came from the cylinder now. Liquid sounds, hissing, bubbling noises. Pumps within the pedestal throbbed to life. Gradually the amber liquid began to drain, the body to skin until its feet touched on the floor. As the lessening fluid exposed the head, tubes released, eye shields retracted. Varina unconsciously stepped back, away from the chamber. There was a brisk cracking noise, a hiss of air pressure, and the sheath of the cylinder began to hydraulically lift. In the dimness of the hall the creature who had been Sidra stood again in the shape in which she had first appeared on earth.

While the creature's eyes were still closed, Varina backed farther away from the pedestal. She was afraid, and ashamed of her fear, and she knelt as if in prayer.

For several minutes Sidra stood unmoving, as if still unaware of her ability to do so. Then, tentatively, the left arm flexed and reached up to caress the smooth head. Varina smiled as she realized Sidra was checking to make sure the hair was gone, that dust-collector she had always disliked. And in that instant she wanted to run over and embrace her and say how glad she was—but that was human. . . . Sidra's arm dropped again and she stood, waiting for the attendants that should be beside her. But no technicians came. Auditory portals flexed, registering the lack of sound. A slight change of expression swept over the face. Slowly, reluctantly, the eyelids parted.

The cinnamon eyes looked out upon the emptiness of the Great Hall, swept it round and from side to side and in despair came to rest upon the small white kneeling figure. For what seemed a long time, Sidra regarded her and then stepped down slowly behind her to form a clear column again. The skin was drying now, beginning to shine. In the thicker atmosphere that filled the room, Varina could hear her softly humming.

"You please me. Of all that we brought to this world, you most please me. If we also brought failure, or if our failure was inevitable, you were no part of it. You will remain here, the most valuable gift of the Delikon: the teacher.

"Do not waste life mourning. Grief is an illness, chaotic, productive of nothing. You will recover. You will live and teach and endure—for you are a Delikon and no Delikon willingly insults the gift of life. There is no more and no less. Go now."

She moved abruptly. Swiftly and with long strides she crossed the hall to stand beneath the spiralway high above. To Varina she gave one last glance and repeated, "Go now. Live for us both. Know joy," bowed her head in farewell, and turned away.

Varina did not move. Silence filled the temple and whispered in her ears.

Then Sidra began to sing. It was a song such as earth had never heard before and would never hear again, a pavane for an alien queen.

Although she had never heard the song before, Varina knew it or recognized it for what it was. And she knew also that neither she nor anything else of this world existed now for Sidra. The birds that were greeting the morning outside fell silent in fear as the monstrous hum filled the air. And Varina rose again and backed away from the singer until she stood in the shadows near the door, ready to flee the death she knew was near.

In the light from the spiralway above her, Sidra stood alone, golden and more beautiful to Varina's eyes than any earthly creature she would ever see. And the song called to her of the beauty of the Delikon, of the House that once was hers, the minds Varina would never touch again, joy that would never be. For the first time she understood Aron: as Aron lost Kelador, so she was losing this.

It seemed to her that she could not endure this loss, that she must join Sidra. But Sidra was already beyond her—for her song had grown in volume and power, if not beyond the endurance of Varina's understanding, beyond the endurance of this fragile body that would now be hers so long as she lived.

As Sidra's song continued, as volume and pitch increased, the floors of the temple began to vibrate, the great columns to hum. Somewhere overhead a piece of masonry shook loose and plunged to fragment on the floor one hundred feet below. The spiral began to spin faster. Refracted darts of light danced madly, and the dust of disintegration filled the air.

Knowing now how it would end, in her human weakness Varina wanted to cry out and beg Sidra to stop. But the Delikon in her knew there could be no other end without shame. She could not ask her to live, a prisoner of the temple's atmosphere, to risk human loathing and extinction.

For the last time the teacher paid homage to her guardian, to her own kind, and it seemed a poor homage to pay this creature of power. She stepped away from the door, toward the singer, and made a formal bow of farewell. There was no lull in the song; the great eyes took her in for a moment and held her, then lifted their gaze to the rotating spiral.

When she saw Sidra raise her head, Varina knew the end was coming. She turned and fled to the door. The metal panel was hot against her hand; the door resisted her, shivering in its frame, the lock failing to release. The song now was so loud that even inside the helmet Varina felt her head would split with pain. Wave after wave of sound pressed against her, disrupting her heartbeat, vibrating through her body. She could hear the walls and windowpanes within the building humming on their own separate frequencies, and she knew her own death was very near.

There was an explosive crack, and from the corner of her eye she saw a crystal column break from the ceiling and shiver into fragments. As it fell there was a second crack, and another column shattered. Three more broke, and still Sidra sang. The ceiling split and then seemed to explode as the denser atmosphere inside rushed out.

With one frantic lunge Varina threw her full strength against the door and felt it open. Above her, as if weakened by the opening of the door, the wall cracked to the roof. She raced across the portico and down the steps, across the plaza into the garden, and down to the river. As she reached the bridge, an abrupt crescendo of sound made her turn and look in time to see the Great Temple fall to crush the queen to silence, to death. There was a roar of gases igniting and flames roared across the rubble.

Twenty-nine

FOR THOSE FIRST few minutes after she had flung away her helmet Varina stood on the river bank and watched the fire. It did not surprise her that she was alone. It did not even occur to her. What had been her reality these past ten days had been of so bizarre a quality that the absence of frightened or curious onlookers now seemed not unusual. With the still clarity of shock, she watched a herd of tiny temple deer race in panic past the tombs and down along the ruin. Two ancient cedars in what had been the temple courtyard were torching. With a great muffled roar a huge steel tank rose up weightlessly from the flames and fell, crashing through the roof of the t'kyna's private residence. The building seemed to *oof!* with the impact; the windows shattered, and flames licked out. She looked at the billowing smoke and then at the mountains beyond. The mountains, like the gardens, the sunrise, and the river, had not changed at all. And that surprised her.

The first of the fire equipment arrived without her noticing it. After a few futile attempts to approach the hotly burning ruins, the crews began wetting down the surrounding area. There was a surge of people around her, touching her, embracing her, shouting incoherently over the roar of the fire. She was aware of them only when they blocked her view of the flames and she had to push past them to see.

A tall man came and stood beside her. He kept the others away, silenced their questions. She did not look at him, but she was grateful for his kindness. He appeared to understand that her vigil would not end until all that was in the temple was ashes.

When it was, and only charred smoking stones remained, with the silent tact of a Delikon he walked with her over the footbridge that led back to the palace. And the people stepped aside and let them pass in silent respect. Not until Alta and Jason, waiting on the opposite river bank, called out her name and his did she truly see him.

"Aron? Is Varina all right?"

She neither faltered nor flinched. That would be unseemly in the presence of others. So this was what Alta and Jason had been talking about these past days when they said the war was over. He was here. It was ended. And it had begun.

Thirty

IN A NORTHERN LAND stood a palace encircled by the arms of a gentle river. To the east were temples; to the west, cypress-guarded tombs. A white road led to the river and crossed the high bridge.

In the palace gardens were reflecting pools and an enclosure for tigers. Three old friends walked in the garden and spoke of days that had been.

The tigers heard them coming. Behind their moat, on sun-warm rocks, the cats awoke to yawn and stretch and wait with lazy burning eyes. From the hill beyond the temples came the shouts of children playing. When the shouts were pitched high enough, peacocks would scream defiant answer.

From west to east, high above the mountains, a brilliant object streaked across the sky, slicing through cirrus clouds, trailing a wake of white vapor and silence.

Varina's face went still. She watched the ship until distance dwindled it to a bright speck that turned and circled north and sank behind the mountains.

"What is it?" said Alta. "Why does it frighten you?"

"I am not afraid," said Varina, and it sounded like a prayer.

"It's just a meteor," Jason said reassuringly. "Nothing scary."

"Forgive me . . ." said Varina and she took their hands. For a moment her strange cinnamon eyes scanned first Jason's face, then Alta's, as if she had never seen them before and might never see them again, and then she kissed them both. "You have never disappointed me," she said and, turning, ran down across the lawn and disappeared behind the hedge of the topiary garden.

"Are you coming back?"

She heard Jason call, but she could not answer because she did not know.

ABOUT THE AUTHOR

H.M. Hoover was born near Alliance, Ohio. "I came from a long line of farmers, teachers, and an occasional minister," she says. Ms. Hoover has traveled extensively in the United States and has had ample opportunity to pursue her interests in natural history, history, and archaeology. The author of *Children of Morrow, The Lion's Cub,* and *Treasures of Morrow,* she lives in New York City.